only for you

THE LICK SERIES
BOOK 3

only for you

THE LICK SERIES

BOOK 3

NAIMA SIMONE

Entangled Publishing, LLC
2614 South Timberline Road
Suite 109
Fort Collins, CO 80525
Visit our website at www.entangledpublishing.com.

Scorched is an imprint of Entangled Publishing, LLC.

Edited by Tracy Montoya
Cover design by Cover Couture
Cover art from Shutterstock

Manufactured in the United States of America

First Edition December 2016

entangled
scorched

To Gary. 143.

Chapter One

Grunts. The wet suction of metal slamming into flesh and jerking free. The dark crimson splash of blood. The tangy, wet-penny scent of it heavy in the air.

The large, meaty fist crashed into Killian Vincent's jaw, and his head snapped back. He welcomed the hot blaze of pain. Loved it.

More.

Another blow to his jaw. A red haze dropped over his vision.

The clang of a steel door closing. The stygian darkness. The walls and ceiling inching closer...closer...sucking the air from his lungs. "I can't breathe. I'm going to die..."

He shot his arm out, the swing a bit wild, a lot desperate. But accurate. Bone connected with his knuckles, transmitting a jagged, almost pleasurable vibration up his arm, into his shoulder.

Yes. More.

His opponent, probably some frat boy slumming it for shits and giggles, grinned. "What's the matter, bitch?" he sneered, flashing a cocky smile that had probably cost his parents thousands. "You look a little tired there. Not used to having your ass kicked?"

Less talk. More punching. As long as flesh connected with flesh and pain white-washed thought, the memories didn't choke him.

He cranked his jaw from side to side, then ducked the fist flying toward his throat. Killian slammed his own into the preppy, wannabe badass's kidney. The fresh meat doubled over, and Killian jacked up his knee, ramming it into the guy's face. Blood spurted, splattering Killian's skin and the dirty cement floor of the abandoned Boston warehouse. The crowd surrounding the makeshift ring roared, the sight of so much blood rousing them into a fury. But Killian backed off, balancing on the soles of his booted feet.

C'mon, man. Fight, he silently urged the preppy. The demons in his head hadn't quieted yet, though their noise had muted some since the fight began. But not completely.

The guy stumbled backward, dropping his guard and clutching his bleeding nose. Growling, Killian advanced and let loose with a flurry of punches to the abdomen, chest, and finally, to the jaw. The other man dropped to the ground, his head bouncing hard off the crimson-spattered cement.

Get up, damn it. He wasn't ready to call it quits. This bout hadn't lasted nearly long enough. The memories still lurked in his head, flickered in the shadows.

When the preppy didn't move after several long moments, Killian strode out of the makeshift ring in disgust. When the asshole eventually came to, it was going to be a long, painful ride back to Beacon Hill or whatever rich part of Boston he'd traveled from.

The yells and shouts of the hyped-up crowd rose to a deafening din, bouncing off the bare walls of the warehouse. Men in business suits or jeans and T-shirts. Women in short, designer dresses or cutoffs and skimpy tops. Rich, poor, black, white, gay, straight. Watching one man beat the shit out of the other was equal opportunity entertainment.

Killian ignored them all, pushing through the mob of bodies. They parted for him, but more than a few women grabbed at his arms or stroked a hand over his chest, grazing his nipple piercing. If he stopped, they would all issue the same invitation: *Want to fuck?* Some of the women came to these things specifically to ball a fighter. But none of them interested him.

Not that he wasn't down to screw.

Fighting and fucking... They were the only things that quieted the incessant drone buzzing under his skin and the memories clawing at the inside of his skull.

"Vincent." The harsh, smoke-blackened voice halted him as he snatched up the T-shirt he'd dumped in the back corner before his fight.

Glancing at Rick Lester, the organizer of these underground fights, Killian dragged his shirt over his head before answering. "Yeah."

"You keep knocking 'em out that quick, people get disgruntled about not getting their money's worth. And it's becoming hard to find someone to go up against you."

Killian shrugged. "I don't know what you're getting at. I'm not taking a dive for anyone. So get better opponents."

Even in the dark warehouse, Rick's eyes gleamed like the sly ferret he resembled. "Tomorrow night. I can line you up with Ben Trainor. What'd you say? You up for it?"

Ben Trainor. The man had a reputation for being brutal, merciless. Known for fighting dirty.

Perfect.

"Yeah. I'll be here," Killian growled.

Half an hour later, a roll of cash in his pocket, he handed his keys to a valet and looked up at the huge, converted brick warehouse that dominated most of the block in Boston's upscale Leather District.

Lick.

The club he and his best friends, Rion Ward and Sasha Merchant, owned together. The three of them had come from nothing—broken homes, screwed-up parents, the Irish mob. Through jail, getting shot…and worse…they'd survived and finally escaped a world that would've eventually left them dead or back in the hell also known as prison. Now they were legitimate businessmen, owners of Boston's newest and most exclusive aphrodisiac club. They were their own men, their loyalty to no one but each other and the two new women in Rion and Sasha's lives.

Anger, bright and hot, flared inside him as he turned into the side alley bordering Lick. Women and loyalty. Not his strong suit. Being narced out to the cops by one didn't foster trust.

Unlocking a steel door, he stepped inside a tiny, dimly lit vestibule. Like every night, sweat popped out on his forehead, neck, and arms. His chest constricted, as if a vice grip slowly tightened and tightened, compressing the air out of his lungs. Gritting his teeth so hard, his jaw twinged in protest, he punched in a five-digit code on the lit pad next to the second door. As soon as the light flashed green, he pushed through, entering his office with a loud expulsion of breath, followed by a greedy gulp of air.

He stood still on the other side of the entrance, eyes closed, hands curled into fists at his sides. *In. Out. In. Out.* He drew air in his nostrils, blew it out through his mouth until his body relaxed, and bit by bit, the panic eased its claws out of his psyche.

The two doors with the coded entry were added security

measures, but goddamn, every night, he suffered a measure of hell just to enter the building.

Fucking claustrophobia.

Opening his eyes, he rolled his shoulders back and cracked his knuckles. The blissed-out moments the fight had given him were already ebbing. Growling, he stalked to his office bathroom, showered quickly, and changed into a black, long-sleeved shirt and black pants. With efficient movements, he swiped a rubber band off his desk and gathered his dark, shoulder-length hair into a bun at the back of his head.

A knock sounded at the door, and a glance at the bank of monitors on the far wall revealed who stood on the other side. He crossed the room and pressed a button on the underside of his desk, and the lock disengaged. Sasha Merchant entered the office, his blue-gray gaze locating Killian and scanning him from head to toe, pausing on the small bruise he felt darkening along his cheekbone. Wasn't the first, wouldn't be the last.

"You should see the other guy," Killian drawled. A cliché, but, in this case, definitely true.

Sasha grunted, striding across the room. "You just getting in?"

"Yeah." Killian scrubbed a hand over his chin and jaw, hair bristling against his palms. He'd passed five o'clock shadow about twenty-four hours ago. Narrowing his eyes, he studied the other man. Noted the taut set of his shoulders, the grim set of his mouth. "Why? Is something wrong?"

Rion and Sasha understood Killian's need to fight, to release the tension, ease the noise. They didn't give him shit the two or three nights he arrived at Lick after the doors had opened. In charge of security, Killian had hired a professional and skilled team, and they were more than capable of handling any issue that arose in his absence. Still, if Sasha was in Killian's office—instead of out in the club or up in The

Loft—wearing an expression that promised an ass-beating, then there was a problem.

"What is it?" Killian asked again, bracing himself for anything from drug dealers in the club, to overzealous guests trying to snap pictures of celebrity guests in the VIP lounges, to reporters sneaking in and trying to sniff out rumors about a "sex club."

Not that the rumors were false, but they didn't need the press hounding the clientele who paid obscenely for discretion and privacy. The second level of Lick—The Loft—offered a safe haven for certain members to indulge in and enjoy their particular desires and fetishes. And the last thing those members wanted—or Killian, Rion, and Sasha needed—were photographs and articles written in detail about the aphrodisiac club on the second floor of Lick.

Sasha nodded toward the monitors behind them. "Pull up the camera behind bar two."

A sense of dread rose in his chest as he turned around and faced the console behind his desk. With a few taps on the keyboard, he brought up the live feed from the cameras behind one of the long, glass bars that dominated each side of the converted warehouse.

"The one on the far end near the dance floor," Sasha instructed.

Another tap, and a view of one of their registers, Point Of Sale systems, and bartenders filled the screen. For several long seconds, he scrutinized the images. The bartender filled glasses and rang up drink orders. She didn't pocket money or over-pour alcohol. So she wasn't who or what Sasha needed him to see.

Killian shifted his attention to the people filling every available space around the bar. Guy with too much gel and obviously too little game chatting up a woman who wore a frown that practically screamed "kill me now." Two women sipping cocktails and giggling together. *Hmm*. They appeared a little on the young side. He needed to have their IDs double-checked to ensure they were actually twenty-one. Another group of women gathered in a tight semi-circle. One, a blonde who seemed vaguely familiar, tipped her head back, laughing. The dark-haired woman on the right lifted her head, smiling directly into the camera…

Holy. Fuck.

The hair was longer, the makeup more understated than he remembered. But those lips. Goddamn, those lips. They hadn't changed, and he could still easily recall how they were slow to smile, but when they did, the sight had filled him like helium in a balloon, lifting him higher and higher. How they opened so willingly for his tongue, for his kiss.

And the eyes. *Christ*. Those deep, heavily lashed, purple eyes had glittered in anger, shined in laughter, darkened with lust, and gleamed with love.

Or so he'd thought. The love had been a lie. A cruel, fucked-up lie.

No, regardless of the different length of hair and amount of makeup, he knew that face.

It was the face of the woman who'd once owned every piece of his heart.

The woman who had betrayed him, sent him to hell, and damn near destroyed him.

Chapter Two

Sometimes hanging with the girls for a night out was just the thing needed to lift a person's spirits.

Gabriella James tipped her bottle of Sam Adams to her mouth and drank deeply, throwing a glance at her cackling, tipsy cousins. She swallowed a sigh along with another gulp of beer.

Then sometimes a person just wanted to sit at home with a bowl of M&M's and the latest season of *Game of Thrones* playing on DVD. Alone. Well, except for her beloved Tyrion. Between him and *The Hobbit*'s Thorin Oakenshield, she'd so be the filling in that dwarf sandwich.

But after being away from home for almost five years, she would've been a Debbie Downer to reject her cousin and sister-in-law's invitation to treat her to a few celebratory drinks. Gabrielle snorted. These bitches had passed "a few" about three tequila shots and a raunchy twirl on the dance floor ago. They were well on their way to fucked up—which left Gabriella, with her two beers, the designated driver.

Fuuuun.

Still, she couldn't completely blame a guilt trip on her reason for being in the packed converted warehouse. Curiosity and masochism comprised the other 75 percent.

Curiosity about the seemingly popular club that hadn't existed when she'd left Boston all those years ago.

And masochism because she'd come here hoping to catch a glimpse of its owner.

One of its owners anyway.

She should've known nothing—not less-than-stellar beginnings, jail, or the Irish mob—would've separated Rion Ward, Sasha Merchant, or Killian Vincent.

Killian.

The familiar ache in her chest pulsed a bright, neon red at just the mental whisper of his name. The man she'd loved from the first time she'd laid eyes on him at nineteen years old, when he'd stalked into her uncle's bar on her first night—illegally—serving drinks. The man she'd never stopped loving.

The man who hated her.

Not that she blamed him. After all, she'd ratted him out to the police. He'd been arrested. Had ended up going to jail.

Yeah, Killian despised her for betraying him.

Didn't matter that she'd committed the unforgivable sin to save his life.

She lifted the bottle to her mouth and sipped the beer without tasting it. The mundane actions offered her something else to concentrate on rather than an ill-fated love, but did nothing for the nerves twisting in her belly. She huffed out a silent, humorless chuckle. Pathetic. She was apparently pathetic and stupid as well as into emotional self-flagellation.

One would think she'd learned her lesson about dreams coated in the glitter of gullibility and youthful, *foolish* optimism. Blissful couples with their happily ever afters belonged in places like Chestnut Hill and Newton with their gorgeous mansions, obscenely large salaries, and carefully manicured lawns and lives. They definitely didn't apply to dive bar waitresses, sometimes bartenders, and their mobbed-up boyfriends from South Boston who barely earned enough to cover rent for a cramped one-bedroom apartment. Hell, her mother, with her many boyfriends and rare moments of happiness, had proven that. Why had Gabriella believed she would be any different?

"Your man did good, didn't he?" Her cousin, Janelle, nudged Gabriella's arm, nearly knocking her beer out of her hand. The tipsy blonde's Long Island Iced Tea fared just fine, though.

"He's not my man," Gabriella murmured, not bothering to pretend she didn't know to whom her cousin referred. For two years, he had been the axis her world revolved on. There wasn't any point in denying it now. "And yes," she added, switching her bottle to the opposite hand and out of Janelle's reach. "This is nice."

And wasn't that the understatement of the millennia? Lick… Lick was nothing short of amazing. She surveyed the walls of exposed brick with its sensual, framed black-and-white photographs, the two glass and chrome bars with their impressive stocks of top-shelf alcohol. She'd worked as a bartender in one of the trendiest and hottest clubs in Los Angeles before returning home and recognized the cost of the premium alcohol they offered. But from the sheer number of people jockeying for rare space around the bars, gyrating on the dance floors, and crowding every available table, chair, and red and blue couch, she supposed the club could afford every luxury item she'd glimpsed. From the liquor, to the DJ she recognized as one of the most talented and in-demand in the country, to the cordoned-off VIP lounges with their crimson drapes and celebrity faces.

Pride burst inside her like a bright, colorful firework. Jamie Hughes, head of the Irish mob's notorious O'Bannon gang, had only seen Killian as a pair of fists to torture those poor souls who'd been stupid enough to fall on the mob boss's bad side by not paying up on loans or gambling debts. But Killian—big, brooding, quiet—had been so much more. Loyal, insightful, incisive, and brilliant. It'd been that man she'd fallen so hard in love with, even though he'd been a mob enforcer when she'd first met him. No, that part of his life had scared her—she'd hated it—but for the man she adored, she'd been willing to love him out of it, offer him a glimpse of a future with her, marriage…a family. She'd accepted that there'd been this anger that had always simmered just under his skin. Given his rough childhood and history, she'd understood. She'd also acknowledged that he could be volatile and so stubborn… which had led to the decision that had shattered them forever.

But still…this place.

Yeah, Killian had definitely "done good."

What she'd always hoped and desired for him.

"Nice? That's all you got is *nice*?" Even in her inebriated state, Janelle seemed to read Gabriella's mind. "Gabby, I think the west coast might have jaded you. This right here," she flung an arm wide, the expansive gesture including the interior of the club, "is the shish," she slurred.

"Right," Gabriella drawled. "The shish." Goddamn it, if Janelle couldn't even pronounce "shit", Gabriella was going to be pouring her cousin into her car. She gave the two women another half hour, tops. Then she was dragging them out the front door, even if it had to be by their hair. Hell, it wouldn't be the first time.

Besides, she glanced down at her watch, it was already 11:45, and she hadn't caught a glimpse of Killian. Maybe he wasn't here tonight. And maybe she should just count her blessings and cut her losses… She wasn't even certain what her plan or goal had been coming here tonight. Get a peek at him, then make a break for the door, not returning for another five years? Seek him out, say "hi," and hope he wouldn't have her ass kicked out of the club? Either option ended up with her leaving skid marks on the sidewalk.

Yep, cutting her losses was sounding better and better.

She remained planted on the barstool.

"And who are you looking for?" Janelle sing-songed, poking Gabriella in the arm, giggling.

"Oh, you already know the answer to that question," her sister-in-law, Wendy, piped up from the other side of her cousin. "You don't really think she came out here just for us, do you?" She smirked, arching an eyebrow high. Damn. Gabriella should've remembered her sister-in-law always released the reins on her inner mean girl when drunk. Wendy snickered. "If you knew what your man's been up to, I don't think you'd be so gung ho to see him."

Ignoring the urge to shout *"He's not my man!"* and give the women more ammunition, she instead focused on the last part of the comment. "What are you talking about, what he's been up to?" A sliver of unease slipped between her ribs. Didn't this club mean Killian had gone legit? Was out of the mob?

Again, Wendy laughed, the edge to it a clear warning Gabriella wasn't going to appreciate the other woman's answer. "Aside from tearing up the underground fighting scene, rumor has it that Killian Vincent has been"—she paused, grinned—"tearing up the sheets, too. Like, *hard*."

Pain stabbed Gabriella like a hot poker straight to the heart. It'd been five years since they'd been together— of course he hadn't been a monk. He didn't owe her any loyalty. She had firsthand knowledge to how "hard" in the bedroom—or in the kitchen, or the living room, or a dark corner in the storeroom of her uncle's bar—Killian could be. He'd introduced Gabriella to an eroticism she'd never experienced...and hadn't since him. He'd been the first to push her sexual limits, teach her how the bite of pain could intensify pleasure, heighten it. Been the first to take her ass and make her love it. Crave it.

The first…and the last.

"Wendy," Janelle hissed. "Shut up."

"What?" Wendy held up the hand not holding a drink, widening her eyes. "If she sticks around long enough, she'll hear the gossip, too. Besides, we're family, so she should hear it from us."

Janelle shoved her face into Wendy's, their noses almost bumping. "It's none of our bus—"

"Be right back. Bathroom." Gabriella launched off her stool before either woman could object or offer to come along. Space, she needed some space. From the cattiness. From the memories of her and Killian. From the images of Killian and other, faceless women.

As if the hounds of hell snapped at her heels—including one wearing Wendy's features and containing a knowing, leering gleam in its glowing, red eyes—Gabriella weaved a path through the crush of bodies toward the back of the club and the restrooms. She checked the urge to pull a *Hulk, smash!* and, gritting her teeth, steadily continued forward, her focus centered on the Exit sign at the rear of the warehouse. As she skated across the dance floor, someone bumped into her shoulder, almost knocking her over.

"Damn," she mumbled, quickly righting herself before turning and glaring a fist-sized hole into the back of the offender's head. Not that the guy seemed to care or notice that he'd almost made her ass meet the floor. "What a jerk…"

Her voice trailed off as a door on the far wall opened, and a tall, wide figure stepped out. Shadows and distance obscured his face, but that didn't stop a low hum of electricity from entering her body. That current hadn't sizzled in her blood in five years. She waited, feet rooted to the floor. A stampede of people could come crashing toward her, but she wasn't moving. Not until she saw his face. Not until she knew for certain...

Oh God.

Killian.

Her heart pummeled her chest, like a beast trying to fight its way free of its cage. Thunder crashed and roared in her ears, deafening her to everything but the harsh rasp of her breath.

She should've been prepared—she'd come here hoping to catch a glimpse of him. But God, had she been naive. Nothing could've equipped her for this moment, this first look at this man who had claimed her at the age of nineteen with his particular brand of lust and love. He'd branded her, had seared *Mine* onto her soul, and time and distance couldn't change that fact.

It also couldn't change her body's ingrained reaction to just the hint of him. The hope of him. The impact of him.

Desire thickened and slid through her veins like hot, delicious molasses, swelling her breasts, tightening her nipples, before winding south and pooling between her legs. Her chest rose and fell, her breaths already deepening. When was the last time she'd experienced that painful but sweet ache? No, she hadn't been celibate in the years since she'd left Boston, but no man but him had ever incited this throb that rode the razor-sharp edge of pain and bliss. No other man could have her body readying to be stroked, penetrated, and pleasured with just a look.

No man but Killian.

Greedily, she devoured him. The big body that seemed to hum with a vitality and barely leashed frenetic energy—an energy that reached out to her even halfway across a packed warehouse, as illogical as that sounded. The wide shoulders and chest that would've had Bill Belichick selling his soul to have on the Patriots' offensive line. The narrow, taut waist that her fingers had dug into, her thighs had embraced. The thick, muscled legs that reminded her of powerful, marble columns charged with supporting massive structures.

Joy, sadness, and lust wrapped her in their freezing, paralytic embrace. She couldn't move, could barely breathe as he stalked toward her. Even with his brows jacked down in a fierce, dark vee that sent shivers trampling over her skin, and his mouth firmed in a grim, straight line, she was frozen to the spot. He didn't slow in his focused, intent stride; he moved forward as if he expected people to scamper out of the way for him…and they did.

God, if she possessed even an ounce of self-preservation, she would cut a path through the crowd and try to shake him before he reached her. But this was what she'd wanted, right? To see him? To maybe talk to him? Indecision swirled inside her, panic tickling the back of her throat. Yet something more eddied low in her belly, pulsed in her clit, heated her deep inside where no man but him had ever touched. Desire. Arousal. Need.

In a club bursting with people, she burned.

And shook. As he closed in on her, she shook like a shock victim. That face. How many nights had that hard, harshly sculpted, beautiful face haunted her? Like a man stumbling upon a banquet after being denied food for years, she hungrily traced the dark slashes of his eyebrows, the sharp thrust of his cheekbones, the lush curves of his mouth, the solid jut of his jawline. At one time, she'd had permission, the freedom to caress that face, to wake up to it. Now… Now, she had to force her hands to remain down by her sides because trying to touch him would be courting danger. Like sticking her hand into the cage of an angry beast.

Ten feet.

Run, fool.

Six feet.

Oh shit, this is not going to end well.

Three…

He didn't stop. Didn't pause or speak to her. His hard fingers wrapped around her bicep, his expression merciless, and he pulled her after him. Stunned, she followed him. Not that he was giving her much choice.

His broad shoulders filled her vision, blocking out everything and everyone else. Everything but the tight band of his fingers around her arm. Even through the cotton of her long-sleeved, blue shirt, her skin burned, the heat emanating from that one place to her breasts, nipples, her sex. He was touching her—for the first time in years, Killian was touching her again. Didn't matter that it was a grip that radiated his disdain. Her body didn't know the difference…or just didn't give a damn.

Probably the latter.

Moments later, he stopped in front of a door, jabbed in a code on a mounted pad, and entered a room, tugging her behind him. Almost immediately, his hand dropped away from her as if he regretted even those few seconds of touching her. A click, and then a soft glow bathed the area, and she blinked against it, her eyes taking seconds to adjust after a couple of hours of LED lighting.

A dark brown, leather couch, two big, matching armchairs, and a glass coffee table formed an elegant but comfortable-looking sitting area. A dormant fireplace, wooden mantel, and huge, mounted television dominated the far wall. In the corner sat a cherrywood cabinet with several drawers. More of the photographs that hung in the club appeared in this room as well, the sensual, black-and-white prints adding to the intimate atmosphere.

It appeared to be some kind of private room, probably for the VIPs and celebrities when the upstairs booths weren't…

secluded...enough. She could just imagine what probably went on in here. Just as she could imagine what occupied those cabinet drawers. Top of the list: condoms.

"What is this?" She waved a hand toward the room, smothering the swell of jealousy surging inside her like Old Faithful. Too easily, she could imagine Killian's big body covering another woman on that over-size couch. The taut muscles of his back and ass flexing as he pressed against her, drove his cock into her. Without any effort at all, she could envision him sprawled in one of those chairs, his hands buried in the hair of the woman kneeling before him, guiding her mouth up and down his dick. Once upon a time, that faceless woman would've been her—had been her. "You have a playroom in your nightclub? That walks the tenuous line between hot spot and stripper joint."

"VIP room," he corrected from behind her. Paused. "The playrooms are upstairs."

She should hate him for admitting they did have them. If what Wendy claimed was true, he took full advantage of them. And if he hadn't delivered the explanation in that low, deep, coarse voice, she might have dwelled on that resentment. But God, the texture of it—gritty, like a road that had been churned up for repair and had just barely been smoothed over—slid over her skin in an almost rough caress. Yet, something was...off...

"Did something happen to your voice?" she asked. Although years had passed since the last time she'd seen his stunning face, inhaled his rich, dark scent, or stroked his hard, sculpted body, she hadn't forgotten one thing about him. Not the scar that bisected his eyebrow or the mole on his left hip bone, and certainly not his voice. Before it'd been just as deep, as shiver-inducing, as smooth as bourbon—just not so... serrated.

She couldn't see him, but she didn't need her eyes to sense

him. The same body heat that had blanketed her in bed in his shithole of an apartment reached out to her now, urging her to lean back against him. To let it cover her once more. But she remained straight, because that warmth was no longer hers to indulge in. The body—the man—no longer hers to claim.

"Jail happened to my voice," he murmured in her ear, the undercurrents of rage swirling in his voice. "Solitary confinement happened to my voice. Any more questions?"

Jail...solitary confinement. Grief and horror at what he must've suffered bombarded her with relentless fists. Her fault. Guilt was bitter in her mouth. The accusation radiated from his words; he didn't need to say it.

"Killian," she whispered.

"What the hell are you doing here?" he growled, finally circling her and coming to a halt in front of her several feet away. As if he couldn't stand being too close to her.

"In Boston? Or the club?" she hedged. What the hell had she been thinking coming here? That he would open his arms for her to run into? That he would say all was forgiven and welcome her home? Had she believed time would cool his anger? A part of her had. That whimsical, fanciful, the-glass-shoe-is-a-perfect-fit side that time and the pain of loss hadn't completely beaten into submission yet.

Staring into his fierce hazel eyes, at the flat line of his mouth, and the tiny tic of a muscle along his jaw, she called herself ten different kinds of idiot for even harboring that small hope. He hated her.

"Either. Both." He crossed his arms over his chest, his gaze slowly roaming over her. Flames licked everywhere his scrutiny touched. Her mouth, shoulders, breasts, hips, legs. She couldn't prevent the spike of arousal that lit her up like a flare gun.

"My uncle's eightieth birthday. The family's throwing him a party since he's selling the bar. He asked me to come home for it." She hadn't been able to refuse the request of the man who had shown her the only kindness she'd known as a child, even though she was in the middle of the biggest negotiation of her life. In three weeks, she would be opening her own bar after years of tending someone else's.

But she couldn't forget all her uncle had done for her, what he'd been to her. When her mother would've drafted her into the world's oldest profession at eighteen, Uncle Garrett had given her a job in his pub, even though she hadn't been twenty-one and legally old enough to serve drinks. Still, he'd granted her independence and freedom. With dementia slowly but steadily pilfering his memories, she couldn't resist coming home. Especially when this might be one of the few times left that he would recognize her.

"My cousin and sister-in-law brought me here tonight."

Again, that deliberate perusal with those hooded hazel eyes. A tingle of apprehension joined the desire. "And when you agreed to walk in this club, did you know I owned it?"

Lie. A sense of self-preservation screamed at her to lie. Handing him the knowledge that she'd purposefully sought him out would be tantamount to an animal exposing its vulnerable neck to a voracious predator...

"Yes," she confessed. "I knew."

"Did you lose your mind in the last five years?" he murmured, cocking his head to the side. "You'd have to be a goddamn fool to return to Boston, much less here, after what you did. And you were a lot of things, Gabriella, but never a fool."

Gabriella. Not Gabby. She'd never be Gabby for him again.

Gabby had been the woman he'd curled his big body around and held through the night. Gabby had been the woman he'd introduced to the dark ecstasy of dirty, mind-shattering sex. Gabby had been the woman he'd protected, pleasured…loved.

But Gabriella was the woman who'd ratted him out to cops. Had left him with a broken voice and a stone heart… If there was one there at all. For her, at least.

"No one knows it was me," she said, voice quiet. "No one but you." She'd committed a cardinal sin in their world. Her violation couldn't be washed away with a litany of Our Fathers, Hail Marys, and Acts of Contrition. That she'd just been trying to save his life wouldn't grant her absolution.

Her uncle's bar had been a popular spot, and guys from all over their neighborhood dropped in. Including members from several of the mob families, not just the O'Bannons, the gang Killian had belonged to. One night, she'd been restocking in the storeroom and overheard a conversation outside of the door about an ambush, betrayal, and murder. The location was at a meeting the next night between the First Street Gang and the O'Bannons. At that time, the two Irish families had established a tenuous truce over territory and the rackets run on those streets, but it'd only been established for six months. And according to what Killian had informed her, the scheduled meeting was supposed to help further cement the truce. But from what she'd overheard, a truce was no longer on the table. Betrayal was, and the targets were the O'Bannons attending the meeting—including Killian, who, as an enforcer, planned on being there as protection for Jamie Hughes.

She'd immediately gone to Killian, needing to alert him about the ambush, to maybe prevent him from going to the meeting. But hotheaded and loyal to a fault—and in spite of her pleas—Killian had rushed headfirst into the trap, determined to warn and protect Jamie and the other gang members. Panicked, terrified he would lose his life, and desperate, she'd done the one thing that would save him. She'd called the police and told them about the meeting.

The day after he'd been arrested, she'd gone to the jail,

tried to see him and explain, but he'd refused to come to the visiting room. The same thing happened the second, third, and fourth time she went. She'd even written him a letter. But nothing. Eventually, she'd had to accept that he didn't want anything to do with her. Refused to forgive her.

So, she'd left Boston, grief and pain driving her across the country. Grief and pain because the man she'd loved despised her for her betrayal. She was leaving again, right after her uncle's birthday party in a couple of days. She would return to L.A. Back to the estranged, lonely, but safe existence she'd lived for the last half decade.

"Killian, I…" she whispered. Paused. Slicked the tip of her tongue over her suddenly dry lips and tried again. "Killian, I'm sorry."

Lame. The apology sounded lame to her own ears, and from the sharp slash of his hand through the air, it seemed he thought so, too. He prowled forward, eliminating the space between them. At the last moment, her survival instincts decided to make an appearance, and she shifted backward. But too little, too late. Before she could draw her next breath, he was on her.

His hands slammed down on either side of her head, caging her between the wall and his tall, wide frame. He pressed his hips against hers, and oh God, the long, thick length of his cock wedged against her belly. She couldn't hold back her whimper. Not when hunger ground inside her like a twisting screw. Her pussy spasmed so hard it almost hurt, damn near begging to be filled, stretched, and branded again. His solid chest pressed against the palms she'd lifted at the last second. Holy shit, were those…nipple rings under his shirt?

"Sorry?" he murmured just above her mouth. So close she could taste the flavor of his breath. "I don't want your damn apology. The only thing I want is you out of my club. Out of my life. Again."

Chapter Three

He was in hell.

And Gabriella James was his horned, devilish tormentor.

Killian curled his fingers into fists, his knuckles grazing the thick, black strands that waved around her flushed, gorgeous face. Soft blasts of her fruity-scented breath puffed against his mouth, and he fought not to swipe his tongue over his bottom lip to taste it. Struggled not to lower his head and gorge on her.

That greedy need urged him to raise his head, demanded he insert distance between them before he surrendered to that craving. Clenching his jaw, he stepped back enough to take her arm and whip her around. Her palms flattened against the wall, her long fall of silken hair hiding her face. Good. He didn't want to stare at her red-painted, lush lips that tempted him with memories of how they'd molded to his, been so pliant for him, so eagerly parted for his tongue, fingers, and cock. He didn't want to peer into those soft lilac eyes that pleaded with him for…what? Forgiveness? He closed his own eyes, his fingers curling into tight fists. At one time, he'd only needed one glance in that beautiful gaze to give her anything. His body. His protection. His heart. Now?

He had nothing to give.

"Do you know what I thought about the seven hundred and sixteen days I spent in that cage?" More specifically, the thirty days he'd suffered and damn near lost his mind while in solitary confinement. "Every kiss. Every time you let me in your bed, let me slide under the covers and suck those gorgeous tits and tongue that pretty pussy. Every time you let me put you on your hands and knees and take you before having that tight ass. Every time you let me fuck you like an animal, but you never looked at me like one." He forced his arms to his sides but allowed his mouth the small touch he refused his hands. Inhaling her familiar—and resented— wildflower and rain scent, he leaned forward, his lips grazing the shell of her ear. "Every time you smiled when I walked through the bar door, your face lighting up like I alone made you happy. Every time you took my hand in front of everyone, unashamed to claim me. Every time you said you loved me," he whispered. "And then you know what I thought of?" he asked, forcing steel into his voice. Her black strands brushed his mouth in a pseudo-kiss as she gave her head an almost infinitesimal shake. "Then I thought of payback. How I could make you pay for each lie you said with your mouth, your eyes, your body. Make you pay for the betrayal that stole two years of my life." He paused. Then, "Turn around."

After a long hesitation, she slowly pivoted, but he didn't move back. Common sense and his anger ordered him to shift away, insert space. Sex had always been their flashpoint—the first night he'd seen her at her uncle's bar, he waited until her shift ended and followed her out. An hour later, they'd ended up in his truck, with his face buried between her thighs. So yeah, wisdom argued that touching her would be a monumental mistake. But as she turned, and her hip nudged his dick, and her arm stroked his chest, lust momentarily hijacked reason, and he just checked the primal urge to shove her to her knees, cover her, plaster his chest to her back, bracket her thighs with his, and plunge balls-deep inside her. His flesh hardened to the consistency of a steel beam, totally on board with the idea.

But then he remembered.

Remembered the bite of the cuffs around his wrists for the first time in his life.

Remembered the taunts of the detectives of how "she'd" given them every detail of where to find him and the rest of the "thugs." Remembered, as the realization of who "she" was dawned, how the grief, desolation, and rage had imploded inside him and painted the bland walls of the interrogation room until they resembled an emotional abstract art piece.

Remembered the clang of the jail cell doors closing behind him. And how the first black-tipped claws of hysteria had sank into his psyche, tearing his mind apart with panic and an animal's desperate, wild fear.

Could still feel the blaze of the first scream over his vocal cords as it ripped from his throat when that door shut behind him, sealing him in that tiny 6 x 9 hole for twenty-three hours of every day.

He stared down into her beautiful, deceitful face…and remembered.

Rion had once asked him if he'd known the agony Gabriella would bring, would he have still loved her. His answer had been yes then, and it was yes now. Because if he hadn't experienced the joy and freedom of loving her, the pain wouldn't have shredded him. And then he might be standing here, looking down into her lovely face, considering lowering his guard, contemplating forgiveness.

So no, he had no regrets. Because regrets meant being a fool again. Gabriella's fool. And that he couldn't stomach.

"What do you want, Gabriella?" The words rolled from him on a dark, edgy rumble as he backed away from her.

Her thick fringe of lashes fell, hiding her gaze from him. "That night, I was so afraid to come to you with what I'd overheard. But the alternative—hiding it from you...I couldn't do that no matter how much your possible reaction terrified me. And what I feared did happen. You ran right over there, and all I could think of, all I could see, was you hurt, bleeding. Or worse."

She inhaled, the hushed sound echoing in the silent room. "Yes, I called the police. But my one thought was saving your life. I believed it was my *only choice*; otherwise, you could've died. I'd counted on—hoped—the cops' unexpected arrival would bust up the meeting before anyone—you—was hurt. I never imagined you would be charged with or convicted of resisting arrest, and assault and battery on a police officer. My intention wasn't for you to lose two years of your life in jail." She lifted a hand toward him, but after a hesitation, lowered it, shaking her head. "For five years, I've gone over and over that night, trying different scenarios to see what I could've done different. Gone after you myself, maybe called Rion or Sasha. But I panicked. If what I did saved your life, I'm not sorry. But everything else—jail, your pain, your suffering—I am sorry. I wanted you to know that even though it doesn't change anything."

Doesn't change anything? Anger rolled through him like a back draft of fire. He wasn't who he used to be before the night the cops showed up at that meeting and hauled him off to jail. And God, did he mourn that man. That man could love, could enjoy an entire night's sleep without nightmares. That man could enter a closet to select his clothes for the day and not break out into a cold sweat. Doesn't change anything? He'd been altered beyond fixing. And it was her fault.

"Look at me," he ordered, voice soft. When her lashes

lifted, her lilac eyes dark with shadows, he steeled himself against shifting closer. Against feeling anything except the anger. The anger was safe. "I get the 'why.' I get you were scared. But instead of trusting me not to jeopardize what we had by being foolish, you turned me in. Other than Rion and Sasha, you knew me the best. No way in hell would I have rushed into that ambush, guns blazing. Not when that would've meant losing my life instead of spending it with you. But you didn't give me that chance. You didn't give us that chance."

"I did it because I wanted us to have that chance," she whispered. "I—"

"You involved the law—the cops and district attorney that had been trying to destroy the O'Bannons for years. What did you think would happen when they got their chance to haul me to the station? When I didn't play ball with them, they trumped up charges of assault on a police officer and resisting arrest, even though I didn't do either. They sent me to hell for two years."

And as horrifying as that had been, that hadn't been her ultimate sin…

She'd abandoned him.

She hadn't come to the jail to explain why she'd betrayed him. Hell, she hadn't come to see if he still existed. And then, after he'd finally been allowed visitation, Rion and Sasha had informed him why she hadn't been to see him: She'd left Boston. Disappeared. And if her uncle knew where she'd gone, he wasn't telling. Even if the old adage about time healing all wounds was true, and Killian could've somehow absolved her for calling the police, she'd still tossed him aside like their love—like he—hadn't mattered. And that he couldn't excuse. Couldn't forgive.

And he trusted her as far as he could see her with Stevie Wonder's eyes.

"You ever been to jail?" He didn't wait for her answer but pressed ahead, the pressure building and swirling inside his chest forcing the words up and out. He'd never discussed his time in lockup with anyone—not even Rion and Sasha. The irony that she was the first person to hear him talk about it wasn't lost on him. "When that cell door closes behind you the first time, it's like a bullet to the head. Because your soul dies. You can actually feel it curl up and die. And then, when you're in solitary confinement for the first month of your sentence, your mind goes. The darkness, the walls, the smell of piss, shit, and fucking despair closes in on you, crushing you until you can't breathe. Until you start seeing things, losing your sanity with each slow, endless hour that passes. And then there's the noise."

He ground his teeth together, his jaw aching in protest. For a moment, he paused, driving back the avalanche of memories that threatened to bury him under its weight.

"It's never quiet, never any peace. Twenty-four hours of yelling, cursing, laughing. Ever hear a man scream as he's shanked, Gabriella? Scream for his life and for the CO who may or may not make it to him in time? Ever hear a grown man cry out as he's raped?" He ignored her gasp and the tremble of her bottom lip. Just continued, letting the bitterness pour out of him like a twisted faucet. "For two years, that was my life. Always on my guard, never relaxing, sleeping the bare minimum. Ready to fight. I had to become an animal to survive. So yeah, you're right. Your 'I'm sorry' changes nothing. It means nothing," he growled.

"Killian," she whispered, her violet eyes dark with emotion. "I—"

He loosed a bark of hard laughter. "Don't bother saying it again. I don't care that you went to wherever the hell you ran and grew a conscience." *Why you took my heart and trust and shit on them.* "Tell me. How long after I went in did you decide to cut me loose? A month? A week? A day?"

The woman he'd known, had loved, didn't match up to the callous one he described. But then again, he wouldn't have believed her capable of bailing on him as if the two years they'd spent together hadn't meant shit.

Shock crossed her features, quickly chased by disgust. "No," she said, low and fierce. Then, a moment later, softer but no less aggressive, "No." She sucked in a breath, then released it on a shuddering puff. "I didn't 'cut you loose.' How could you think—"

"Think that?" he finished for her when her voice trailed off, and she didn't complete the sentence.

He cocked his head, studying her—the shuttered eyes that used to disclose her every thought, the smattering of pale freckles across her slightly tanned skin, the vibrantly painted, lush mouth. And then down to the perfect handful of breasts covered by a long-sleeved, blue shirt, and lower still to the hips and slim legs encased in dark denim. Nothing flashy or revealing. Hell, compared to the clothes most women wore— or didn't wear—to the club, she could've been dressed in a damn habit.

But aside from her stunning, amethyst eyes, suck-me-deep mouth, sensual features, and tight body, Gabriella had always possessed a confidence, a toughness, an I'm-not-to-be-fucked-with attitude that had been sexy as hell. Some men might find fragility attractive, but her strength had been an aphrodisiac. No, she hadn't—still didn't—need tops or skirts that exposed her tits and ass for the world. Her sexuality had been in how she walked, spoke—hell, breathed.

"We all have our currency, what makes us tick. Mine was you. And until you turned my ass in, I thought I was yours. Until you sold me down the goddamn river then disappeared," he said, his fucked-up voice rougher than usual.

"You were," she murmured. She moved forward, lifted a

hand, her fingers hovering over his chest, and the air stuck in his lungs.

No, his mind shouted.

Goddamnit, yes, the lust—the foolish yearning—inside him roared.

Before Killian could choose a side, her arm lowered. And he breathed again.

"If that were true, nothing in hell could've made you betray me, not trust me," he rasped. *Leave me.*

"I did trust you." A dull red slashed over her cheekbones. A sign of shame? Of remorse? Neither mattered. "I loved you," she whispered.

A bolt of fire roared through him, scorching a path that almost sent him stumbling back a step. "Don't say that to me again," he rasped.

He didn't want to hear those words on her lips. Those lies. His mother had abandoned him, and his father, drunk or high most of the time, might as well have. Besides Rion and Sasha, she'd been the only person he'd let in. Trusted not to hurt him. Believed "I love you" from. What a goddamn fool he'd been…that she'd turned him into.

She shook her head, and what seemed like pain and regret flashed in her eyes. "I wish I could return the years you lost. Or erase all that you've suffered. I wish…" She broke off, briefly closed her eyes. "Forgive me."

"Forgive you," he repeated softly, lifting a hand and circling her throat. The black fan of her lashes rose, and her eyes locked with his. Shock widened them. Then, an instant later, something dark, something wild, entered her stare, a perfect reflection of the greedy need and something rawer, hungrier that lurked beneath the anger and bitterness spinning in his chest. She stilled under his grasp, not even the whisper of her breath echoing in the silent, sound-proofed room. Reflexively, his fingers slightly tightened around her throat, and when she swallowed, the up-and-down motion grazed his palm. Shit, was she aware of how she arched into his hold on her neck? No other woman he'd been with had so eagerly and quickly taken to the dirty sex he enjoyed like Gabriella. She'd turned her ass up for every swat, had shifted her hands behind her for his cuffs, had spread her legs and cheeks open for his every invasion. And had loved it.

As if scalded by both her reaction and the images rolling through his head, he dropped his hand. Shifted backward, placing much-needed space between them.

"You would be better off asking for the moon served up on a platter. There'd be a better chance of getting it," he said, voice flat.

"Payback," she murmured. "You said you thought of payback while in jail. About every time you pushed me to my hands and knees. Every time I let you fuck me like an animal." She stepped forward, eliminating the distance he'd inserted, claiming his breath with each sensuous glide into his personal space. "Here I am. Offering you revenge, payback. Me. However you want me. Any way you want me for the next few hours. Take it. All that I've denied you these past five years. My body. Yours for one night."

She rose on her toes, pressed her breasts against his chest. Her breath brushed his jaw and chin seconds before her soft, lush lips did. He ground his teeth against the back draft of pure need that blew through him at the tender, but sensual caress.

Gabriella tilted her head back, met his gaze.

"Take me."

Chapter Four

"Payback. Take it. All that I've denied you these past five years. My body. Yours for one night."

She heard the words echoing in the room, and part of her balked at saying them. Cringed as she waited for him to reject her. Waited with a pounding heart in hope he would take her up on her offer.

He terrified her. Because he could break her into so many pieces with his passion, she wouldn't be able to find all of them.

And yet, he thrilled her. Because he could break her into so many pieces with his passion, she wouldn't be able to find all of them.

Gabriella shivered, caution warning her not to push. But the erotic shudder reverberating low in her belly and between her thighs shut the caution up with a resounding bitch slap. Her sex clenched, as if preparing itself for his special brand of possession.

"What the fuck are you saying?" he growled. "No."

She should leave it at that. Turn around and walk out of

here. But she couldn't. Desperation, guilt, need...more...kept her there, refusing to accept his rejection.

He wanted her. He could push her away, deny it. But his cock couldn't lie.

Tilting her head back, she stared into his narrowed eagle's gaze. "What did you imagine while in jail? Did you want to use me? Make me pay for every hurt, pain, and betrayal with my body? Did you want to tie me up? Spread me wide? Spank me 'cause I've been a bad girl?"

His wide chest rose and fell on deep, harsh breaths, and he studied her with an intense focus that stroked her cheeks, nose, and lips. Hope and anticipation whispered through her. Oh, yeah, she had him now. "Why?" he rasped.

"Absolution, maybe," she murmured. "Penance. Not just for you, but for me."

And then there was the other, more selfish reason. Five years. Half a damn decade. She missed him. Craved him. After tonight, she'd never have him again. And she was desperate enough to take this opportunity to be with him again, whether in retribution, in a twisted semblance of justice, or absolution of her perceived sin. She'd take it...take one more memory to hoard and tuck away for the years to come.

And it would have to be enough.

She was returning to L.A. and the life she'd built for herself out west in three days. Boston had once been home, but not anymore. And she'd placed down roots in California. Had started over where no one knew her as the daughter of Colleen James, the local hooker. In L.A., no one assumed that when she served drinks, she was also on the menu. Even being Killian Vincent's girlfriend hadn't shed her of that stigma. Now, she stood on her own, didn't lean on her uncle. Now, for the first time in her life, she hovered on the cusp of owning something that was all hers. Even Killian hadn't been all hers—she'd shared him with the O'Bannons. This bar symbolized her independence, her victory over all the shit and shitty people who'd expected her to be slinging drinks and ass for her life. She'd won.

And then, of course, there remained her secret. The one she hadn't been able to reveal to Killian before he'd rushed out the night their lives had imploded.

After her numerous attempts to visit him in the jail and his refusals to see her, cutting her out of his life, she hadn't been able to reveal the identity of the person she'd overheard conspiring with the First Street Gang members at her uncle's bar.

Michael Hughes, the son of Jamie, the O'Bannon gang's boss. The man had turned against his own father, had been willing to cut him and other members down for his own gain. She or her uncle wouldn't have been anything but a footnote in his personal murder book. And, she had no doubt, Michael would have threatened Uncle Garrett to get to her...or worse. So, she'd left, to protect her and her uncle's life, taking her secret with her.

And now, staring into Killian's face, she made the decision to keep that information to herself.

This club, his new life...he'd escaped the mob and their world that had revolved on an axis of violence, despair, and slavery masked as loyalty. Revealing Michael Hughes had planned that hit could possibly send Killian reeling back into the filth he'd washed off. Send him back to the hell that had ruined his voice and two years of his life. It was possible, but could she say for certain? No. This Killian seemed harder, harsher, fiercer, and more controlled than the man she knew. Which made him more unpredictable. Which meant she wasn't risking it or him.

Which meant tonight really was all she would have with him.

"Well, Killian?" she pressed, slipping her fingertips along

his waistband. Dipping between his shirt and pants, caressing his taut flesh for the first time in… She sank her teeth into her bottom lip, biting back a groan. He was hot to the touch, like a furnace burned within him.

Hard, firm fingers wrapped around her hand and removed it from him. Disappointment flashed within her, heavy and dark. No. His answer was still no, and he was sending her away…

"You know what I need. What I want." His hold tightened, not hurting her. God, no. That firm grasp reminded her of what it'd been like between them. Hard. Pressing the limit. Blending the lines between pleasure and the bite of pain. "Do I want you tied up and spread wide? Do I want to spank that pretty ass? Hell yeah. Spank it. Take it. Your mouth. Your tight little body. No part of you would remain untouched. Unfucked. Do you remember how I'd hold you down and tongue you until you screamed, begged me to stop? Did I stop?" He didn't wait for her to reply. Why? They both knew the answer. Hell no. Not until she'd come against in his mouth at least three times. "And I'm not going to stop. Not when I have your mouth full of me. Not when I'm so deep inside you, you'll forget what it is to not have my cock tattooing your pussy. Have you gotten soft in five years, Gabriella? Can you handle it? Whatever I want. No matter how hard or filthy?"

Oh God, yes.

She nodded.

"I need the words," he insisted.

"Yes."

"Then, yeah," he said, lowering his head until their faces were less than an inch apart. All she had to do was slick her tongue across her own mouth to touch his full, lush bottom lip. "One night. Whatever I want and need to get you out of my head once and for all. I haven't been able to push you out, so I'll fuck you out."

His statement vibrated through her like a discordant cord. *I'll fuck you out...I'll fuck you out.* Painful and sweet. He was giving in, but only to be rid of her, then he would forget her, go on living without her as he'd been doing for the last five years. And she had no one to blame for that but herself. Yet, she was willing to pay the price.

His eyes narrowed, and lust rippled through her, beading her nipples, spilling moisture from her sex. She clenched her thighs against the sweet ache. *Careful*, a voice warned. But as if she could feel the seconds of the night ticking by, she shut down that voice with a resounding slam. She could exercise caution when she was back on the west coast. Now, she needed him to brand and be branded.

Slowly, she sank to her knees, her hands lowering to his belt buckle. "Do your worst," she invited, tilting her head back.

Except for a slight flexing of his fingers, he didn't move. She stared up the towering length of his body, lingering on the rock hard line of his jaw, the stern line of his carnal mouth, the slashes of cheekbone, and the faint purple mark above the right one. A bruise, she noted before lifting her regard to his hooded, hazel gaze. That hawk's stare ensnared her, and she paused, waited. But when he didn't speak, didn't stop her, she slid smooth leather through the buckle, unfastened his pants, and lowered his zipper.

Only then did she break the visual entrapment and shift her attention to the body she was exposing. The air in her lungs stuttered, then stalled. Black boxer briefs filled the space between his opened pants. And underneath the cotton... Oh God. Arousal threatened to crush her under its weight. The long, impossibly thick ridge of his cock pressed against the material, the blunt club of his column, the bulbous, flared tip clearly outlined. Goddamn, her mouth watered. It'd been so long. So long since he'd filled her. Since the drag of his heavy length had abraded her tongue. Since the swollen, almost brutish head had penetrated her throat.

With a small groan she couldn't contain, she leaned forward, nuzzled his flesh. Inhaled his musky, earthy scent. Above her he stiffened, and an instant before his hand thrust in her hair, pulling her head back, a thought skittered through her head: You crossed a line.

The caress had been sentimental, personal, not sexual. It'd been a tender greeting, a soft welcoming. She knew it, and from the grip tugging on her hair, raising tiny stings along her scalp, Killian knew it. Soft. Tender. That wasn't what this whole thing was about.

"Hands behind your back," he growled.

She complied, locking the fingers of her left hand around her right wrist and lifting her eyes to his face. Lust blazed down at her, but she didn't flinch from it. She embraced it.

With economic movements, he shoved down his boxers and freed his cock. And holy shit. A freaking apadravya— or happydravya as she'd heard the horizontal piercing that passed through his cockhead called because of the happy times a woman received when the little balls on either side of the bar rubbed her G-spot. Biting back a whimper, she studied the horizontal piercing. She whimpered, a rapt audience as his hand slowly pumped his flesh. He drew his fingers down, down, down the rigid length to the wide base, then retraced his path up, up, up, his fist swallowing the meaty head and the silver jewelry. When the tip reappeared, it glistened with pre-cum. Salty, a hint of spice, and addictive as hell, her sensory memory reminded her. And she craved feeling that bit of silver on her tongue and becoming reacquainted with his flavor.

"What are you waiting for?" she taunted, needing him inside her after so long, even if it was just her mouth. "Give it to me. Hard. I can take it hard," she rasped. She was pushing him, goading him. That part of her that she'd buried this past half decade reared its head again. "Use me. Dirty me. Fuck me so hard that three days from now, the ache will let me know you've been inside me," she half demanded, half pleaded. So when she was back in L.A., she could still feel his possession.

Twin flags of color darkened his sharp cheekbones, and the corner of his mouth curled, twisting his mouth into a snarl that had another rush of liquid heat dampening her panties.

"You think I don't know what you're doing?" he murmured as he continued stroking his flesh. Damn, she hurt for just that small sample of him. "You're trying to top from the bottom. Trying to control how this night is going to proceed. And you know what that'll get you, don't you?" He reached out with his free hand, cupped her cheek, the gentle caress and tone completely belying the hardness of his words. "Answer me," he said, a hint of steel entering his voice. "What will it get you, baby?"

"Fucked," she breathed, her heart thudding against her rib cage like a primitive drum, the same primal beat throbbing in her sex. "It'll get me fucked."

"That's right. Is that what you want from me? Tell me, Gabriella." The hoarse order practically reverberated with lust and impatience, and it was as seductive as his touch. He didn't move, waiting for her answer, granting her a choice even though he'd just said he would determine how their night would go.

Silent, she studied the stark planes of his face, the burning heat in his eyes, the almost cruel sensuality of his wide mouth. "Yes," she breathed. "That's what I want."

A rough growl rolled from his chest as his big hand curled under her arm and guided her to her feet. She stumbled, her legs weak from the arousal coursing through her, but that same hand steadied her, and led her across the room to the couch.

He didn't give her instructions, instead positioned her how he desired...how she desired. Firm, but surprisingly gentle hands bent her over the couch's arm, and she curled her fingers around it. With quick, economical motions, he removed her ankle boots and tossed them aside. He repeated the actions with her pants, stripping them down her legs, and leaving her clothed only in her blue shirt. When he pushed her legs wider with a nudge to her feet, she moaned as cool air brushed the soaked folds of her sex, teased the bared flesh of her ass and the damp skin of her upper thighs.

A hard chest covered her back, and she loosed a long, needy groan at the sensation of Killian's weight, finally, crushing into her, of his hard, unforgiving cock riding the cleft of her ass. Again, his hand encircled her neck, and crying out, she arched into the hold.

"Killian, please," she said on a moan. "It's been so long..."

Her voice trailed off, and like when she'd nuzzled his cock, Killian stiffened behind her. Once more, she'd made the mistake of making this...personal.

"Bend over." His weight disappeared except for the palm planted in the middle of her back. Except for that hand, he didn't touch her. But as fantastical as it sounded, she could feel his scrutiny like a visual stroke over her ass, her spread thighs, her drenched flesh.

She glanced over her shoulder and peered at him through the strands of hair falling over her eyes. A shudder worked its way through her. Raw, intense lust darkened his face as he stared at her exposed flesh. Golden skin pulled taut over his sculpted facial features, emphasizing the full, sexual curves of his mouth. Tension vibrated from him, and the hand not on her spine was curled into a big fist at his side. Underneath the need, something else seemed to be warring inside him. Probably the same battle she'd waged. Reason against insanity. Caution against recklessness. Self-preservation against I-don't-give-a-rat's-ass.

As if sensing her study, his hazel gaze lifted and met hers. Shadows shifted in the bright depths, and she tensed. Waited. Both of them could ease back from the precarious, trembling edge they stood on at this moment. They hadn't gone so far that nothing couldn't be taken back. She could grab her clothes and walk out of this room. They could return to their lives—his here in Boston, continuing to run his successful club, and hers in L.A., opening her new bar.

It was possible...

Killian dropped to his knees, his hands palmed her inner thighs...and he put his mouth on her.

"Oh God." Her head dropped forward as fire barreled through her veins, setting them ablaze, before culminating in the core of her where Killian stabbed his tongue.

She sobbed, her knees buckling at the erotic contact, only the strength of his hands holding her up. So long, so long. The litany replayed in her head like a song stuck on repeat. And the melody...the melody of that song was his greedy growls as he ate her like a man served a buffet after dining on bread and water for years. He thrust inside her pussy in a carnal parody of a kiss, tasting her, torturing her. She clutched the arm of the couch, holding on, seeking some sort of purchase in this sensual storm battering her, tossing her around like a piece of driftwood.

Humming, he licked a path up her sex, his tongue parting her folds with his broad stroke, and found her clit. A cry ripped from her as he lapped at the small bundle, then sucked it. Hard. No mercy. No quarter. Pleasure pounded at her like relentless waves with slivers of pain surfing the crests. She could do nothing but take it, a prisoner to his mouth and her lust. And when his big, blunt finger penetrated her, spreading her in a way his tongue couldn't, touching her in places his tongue couldn't reach, she surrendered. Eagerly.

With abandon.

Jerking her hips, she rode his fingers and his face. He added another finger. Then another. Gritting her teeth against the fire-laced stretch, she opened her legs wider, accepting him. Accepting whatever he gave her. And as his low rumble vibrated over her flesh, adding another level of stimulation, she knew she had his approval. A glow flickered in her chest at the knowledge, and she rolled her hips harder, wanting— needing—another of those signs of praise.

"Please, Killian," she pleaded, not caring that she begged him for that ecstasy only he had ever given her. His answer was to curl his tongue tighter around her clit, suck with a power that had her rising to her toes to escape…make him chase her. God, she didn't know. Everything in her life had narrowed down to one thing: release.

Darkness crept in, blurring the edges of her vision like flames licking and slowly eating away at paper. Electrical currents sizzled down her spine, gathering at the small of her back, tingling in the soles of her feet. Almost there. Oh God, almost there.

One more stroke of his tongue. One more thrust of his fingers, and she would finally…

His mouth and hands disappeared from her body.

Shock pummeled her, and she remained crouched over the couch's arm, certain he would return to her. Finish her. But seconds passed, and though she could still sense his presence behind her, only the cool air over her hot, throbbing flesh caressed her. Confusion careened through her, and underneath, pain from her overly sensitive sex pounded. She still teetered on that slender ledge of orgasm, but she didn't fall—couldn't fall, when only moments ago she'd been set to tumble headfirst over it.

Understanding was slow to come, but it eventually did.

Punishment.

This was her punishment for goading Killian, for trying to wrestle the upper hand away from him.

Straightening, she turned, tugging the hem of her shirt down so it covered her aching flesh and the very tops of her thighs.

"Bastard," she whispered, the unfulfilled pleasure serrating her voice.

He arched an eyebrow and casually wiped his hand over his chin glistening with the evidence of her lust. Never breaking eye contact with her, he slowly licked his fingers clean. And God, if she didn't feel every stroke over her sex, her quivering inner thighs that still bore the phantom imprints of his possessive grip.

"Did you think it would be that quick? That easy?" he asked, the newly roughened tone lending an ominous quality to the question, instead of the gloating she'd expected. He cupped her chin, and swept his thumb over her lower lip, pressing until the tender flesh inside grazed her teeth. "Last chance, Gabriella."

If she told him right now that she intended to leave this room, that she refused to let him touch her, he would let her go. She knew that with every cell of her being. But she didn't head toward the door. She didn't leave. She wanted this—wanted him—too badly.

"I said, do your worst," she whispered.

Heat flared in his eyes, and he dropped his hand away from her face. "Then let's go," he said.

"What about my cousin and sister-in-law?" Turning, she knelt to pick up her pants and boots. "I came here with them. I can't just abandon them or have them wondering what happened to me."

"They've already been taken care of. Leave those."

She whipped around, gaping at him, a boot in one hand and pants in the other. "Excuse me?"

"Leave the clothes," he reiterated.

She shook her head, her grasp on her jeans tightening. "Humiliation wasn't part of this bargain. I'm not walking out of here without any pants on."

A shadow crossed his face even as his lips firmed into a straight line. "Humiliate you? You think I want to give every motherfucker out there material to go home and fuck their fist to? Let them look at those thighs and imagine them wrapped around their waist? Their head? No, Gabriella, my intention isn't to humiliate you," he murmured, the silken tone all the more dangerous. "My sole focus is hustling your pretty little ass next door and upstairs as fast as possible. Whatever you think about me, I'd never place you in harm's way, and that includes exposing you. Now," he lowered his face until she could easily detect the green flecks in his golden eyes. Something flickered in those eyes. The same thing that, for just a moment, softened his mouth so he appeared almost... vulnerable. Hungry. No, no. Need. Like he needed her to walk out of this room with him. But in the next instant, the emotion disappeared behind a shuttered mask. "Are you in...or out?"

She didn't answer. Instead, she dropped the clothes and walked to the door, that brief flash of...whatever accomplishing what the "pretty little ass" and the possessive tone he'd uttered it in couldn't.

The question sent heat spiraling through her, ratcheting the desire that still hummed in her veins. As did his term "upstairs." What the hell did that mean? More specifically, what waited for her upstairs? Anxiety and anticipation knotted her belly, sharpening the razor's edge of the hunger that still had her pussy clenching and releasing, begging for the release that Killian had withheld.

They exited the room, Killian first, his huge, muscled body a barrier between her and the crowd beyond. Not that she'd had to worry. An L-shaped wall blocked them from the interior of the club, granting privacy. In four short steps, Killian paused in front of a section of wall and pressed a button on a panel. Almost immediately, the wall slid open. She blinked. An elevator. The doors had blended so seamlessly into the wall, she hadn't noticed until they parted, the soft light inside casting a short glow.

With a tip of his head, Killian gestured for her to precede him. Her bare feet slid over the carpeted floor of the elevator, and she curled her toes into the surprisingly lush nap. Apparently, Killian, Rion, and Sasha had spared no expense. Or maybe a half-clothed woman in bare feet wasn't an anomaly for this opulent elevator.

The doors closed with barely a hiss, and she surveyed the showpiece. The box was small, but boasted mirrored walls, warm, wood panels, and even a small crystal chandelier. It was elegant, lovely, and almost unexpected in this place that reeked of sin, excess, and indulgence.

"This is beauti—" She broke off, Killian's stiff figure distracting her, cutting off the rest of her compliment. *What the hell?*

Tension fairly vibrated from him, and his big hands curled and straightened, curled and straightened. His broad chest rose and fell on deep, but labored, breaths. Sweat dotted his forehead, and one lone bead tracked a path down his temple to his rock-hard, tensely clenched jaw. Unease flitted through her, and she reached for him, but at the last second, lowered her arm, remembering they weren't about comfort.

"Killian."

He didn't move, his narrowed stare stuck on the wall in front of him as if the map to the Holy Grail was engraved in its glossy surface.

"Killian," she said, raising her voice and inserting a note of steel in it. "Look at me."

A long second passed, but then woodenly, he turned his

head, his hazel eyes dark, the pupils dilated. He stared at her, but somehow she doubted he saw her. Not with that sharp, almost brittle emotion blackening the depths.

Panic. She recognized the shell-shocked, almost animalistic fear. After her mother had been raped by one of her johns under a bridge, she'd been petrified of crossing one. Each time they'd travelled over Longfellow or Tobin Bridge, her mother would seize up, the air would whistle out of her nose, and her knuckles would pale from the death grip on the door or her purse. Killian wore that same sense of terror. But from what? What had triggered it?

With those questions ringing in her head, she didn't allow pride or fear of rejection to keep her on her side of the elevator. The gut-wrenching thought of him—this powerful, strong, dominant man—enslaved by terror had her eliminating the small space between them. She slid between him and the wall, cupped his face and tilted his head down so he had no choice but to meet her gaze.

"Killian," she repeated his name, smoothing the pads of her thumbs over his cheekbones. Her touch was firm as she tried to ground him in the here and now with her, and not in that place of lonely, dark, paralyzing panic. "Baby, look at me. Please." Triumph winged through her when his gaze lightened. It was only the tiniest degree, but at least he was listening to her, seeing her. "Breathe me with me, okay? In." She inhaled through her nose. "And out," she ordered, exhaling through parted lips. "Do it with me, baby. In. Out. In. Out."

Gradually, he followed her example, all that intense focus trained on her, her face, the pattern of their breaths. When the elevator gently bumped to a stop and the doors slid open, the shadows had cleared from his gaze, and the harsh lines around his mouth and eyes had eased. His body remained strung tight, but he'd come back to her.

He'd come back to her.

Jesus. She had to be careful. Too easily she could forget the landmines that lay between them, and convince herself they could have…what? A relationship built on the past? A past riddled with betrayal, resentment, and lust. Yeah, that would make a solid foundation. She'd sold him out years ago to save his life, and now he couldn't ever trust her again.

It didn't matter. Couldn't matter.

In three days, she would leave Boston again, and they could both return to the lives they'd pulled together out of the wreckage. But at least she would have him. Even for a few hours, she would have him.

His hands covered hers and lowered them, striding forward and backing her out of the elevator, his fingers still clasped around hers. The stark darkness had completely dissipated from his eyes, and the frenetic tension had seemed to shift to something else—something calmer, but heavier, hotter. Whatever had happened to him in the elevator had passed, leaving behind the indomitable, invulnerable man who had stalked her across a club then thrown down a dirty, naughty bargain that had her on her knees…literally.

He released her and, with a palm on the small of her back, guided her down a dimly lit hallway. Apparently, the "upstairs" comprised another section of the club. A more private one from the lack of traffic and noise in the empty corridor. She glanced at the old-fashioned sconces that cast a low light over the walls and the floor, as well as the murals depicting a grandfather clock, people in ornate costumes, and a chandelier. At any other time, she would have appreciated the beauty of the gothic-like mural, but Killian had stopped in front of a green door.

Her heart launched for her throat. Feminine instinct warned her that as soon as she walked through that door, there would be no turning back. That what awaited her on the other side would change her. And probably not for the better.

Killian entered the room, then turned and held his hand out.

End it now. Walk out of here, go home, and you'll still have your heart intact…

She placed her hand in his and followed him inside.

Chapter Five

Killian studied Gabriella's slim back, and the slender, curved legs that seemed to stretch for miles from under her blue shirt. The hem barely cleared the bottom of her ass, and every step she took was a torturous tease. He'd already seen her ass, had cupped it, squeezed it as he ate her sweet flesh, but even minutes later, he wanted, craved, more.

God, that pussy. He rolled his bottom lip between his teeth and slicked his tongue over it. He could still taste her. After so many years, he'd convinced himself that she hadn't flowed sweet and thick like the purest honey. That she hadn't been so addictive. He'd almost lost himself between her thighs, would've willingly drowned in her, if he hadn't dragged himself back from the edge at the last moment. She'd accused him of being a bastard for leaving her right on the brink of orgasm, for leaving her hurting. What she didn't know was pulling away from her had punished him as well. He would've gladly offered up his left nut to have her slick, firm muscles squeeze his fingers as she flooded his hand. Have her clit swell and contract against his tongue. Have her screams of completion rain down on him.

It'd been shiny new and so damn familiar. A surprise and predictable. The old Gabriella had never taunted him, pushed him. Not that she'd been meek; it'd been Gabriella's strength that had made her submission so perfect and precious. This slightly older and hardened version of the woman who haunted his memories challenged him with her mouth, eyes, and body. But the taste, the grip of her sex, her immediate, uninhibited response—they were all the same. Just as he remembered.

Where had she been all these years? What had she been doing? Was she okay? Unbidden, the questions flocked his head. He shouldn't care, but gone was the innocence that had somehow still managed to lighten her eyes back then, though she'd seen nothing but the seedier side of life with her mother's lifestyle, his mob connections, and the barrage of people that tracked in and out of Garrett's bar. The purple gaze seemed sharper, watchful, and full of a knowledge that only experience brought. Hard experience. Her wide, full mouth didn't smile.

I miss it.

Again, the thought crept into his head before he could block it. But once there, he couldn't deny it. Gabriella always had a smile for him—one capable of lighting up a room as well as the darkness that grew bigger every day in his chest. He'd walk into her uncle's bar fresh off a night of gambling, stealing, or collecting debts, and she'd look up from whatever table she waited on and given him that luminescent curve of mouth that let him know he was wanted, missed, cared about…loved.

She even walked differently, he observed as she paced the room, arms crossed over her chest. No longer bouncy and fast as if she'd just downed three cups of coffee. Now her steps were measured, slower, like those of someone always ready and prepared to flee or fight. Streetwise. Yeah, that was it. Somewhere in the last four years and eight months, Gabriella had become streetwise.

"What is this? Your own personal playroom?" The question, or rather the slightly defiant tone beneath it, drew him away from his contemplation of her newer mannerisms and demeanor. "My sister-in-law was regaling me with rumors of your reputation."

He didn't immediately answer, weighing how much to tell her. After a second, he opted to confirm only the information the gossips spread. "No, the playroom is another section of The Loft. This is the exclusive, membership-only part of the club. People pay to play up here without judgment or censorship, and with the promise of the utmost discretion and privacy."

"A sex club?" she asked, disbelief rife in her tone.

"Aphrodisiac club," he corrected. "With the exception of anything demeaning or unsanitary, whatever a person finds sexually exciting, we offer."

She scrunched up her nose in an adorable moue. "And I thought L.A. had some kinky shit. Why?"

Los Angeles. That answered the where.

"You really asking me that?" he asked, voice low, saturated with the lust kindled by the rapid-fire succession of memories across his frontal lobe. Gabriella, spread eagle on her bed, helpless to his mouth and fingers. Gabriella, on her knees, swallowing his cock inch by inch. Gabriella, on her elbows and knees, ass in the air, slowly taking him inside that tight back entrance... How many times had he needed to cover her mouth with his hand to keep her screams from waking her neighbors through the paper-thin walls of her apartment? Or had to move them from the squeaking mattress to the floor for the same reason?

Yeah, she more than anyone should understand the draw of having a safe, worry-free place to indulge in fantasy sex.

"And as the owner, do you...play...here often?" she rasped.

He arched an eyebrow. "Do you really want me to answer that question, Gabriella?" he murmured. "Because be careful what you ask for. I'll give you the truth if that's what you really want."

Her eyes narrowed on him, then after a moment, she whispered, "No. I don't think I do."

Good. Because if he did tell her, the masochistic side of him might demand a like answer, and he damn sure didn't want to know that. Unlike Rion and Sasha, one of his vices hadn't been sharing. And though she hadn't been his for years—had she ever?—the thought of another man caressing all that golden flesh had him hungering for another round in a makeshift ring.

"Are you okay?" The softly spoken question jarred him, and he met her concerned gaze. She tipped her head toward the door. "From the elevator. Are you okay?"

And that topic effectively shut down any kernels of curiosity and simmering desire. Doused it like an ice-cold bucket of water over a campfire. Goddamn claustrophobia. Normally, he avoided the elevator like the clap. When he accessed The Loft, he took the back entrance and steps. But in his hurry to get Gabriella upstairs, he'd been willing to suffer the minute in the confining cage. He'd believed he could handle it. And thinking with his dick had him turning into a goddamn, sweating statue in front of Gabriella.

"I'm fine." The clipped words should've warned her off, and for a moment, he thought she would drop it, but again, this was the new Gabriella.

"What happened?" she pressed. "It was a panic attack, right? My mother used to have them." So that's how she'd known how to center him, assist him through it. If he closed his eyes, he could still feel the gentle but firm touch of her hands on his face. Could still feel the deep breaths she'd coached him through. Still spy the concern in her amethyst gaze.

A greasy slide of shame slithered through his veins. He hated—detested—that she'd seen him weak. Goddamn fragile. Some people came out of jail and were able to put the time behind them, but Killian couldn't. Not when entering his office every night reminded him of that hell. Now his fear was the gift that kept on fucking giving.

"I don't like enclosed spaces," he growled, unbuckling his belt. He needed to distract her…distract himself. He'd come here to lose himself in her, not lose his shit.

"Oh, baby, I'm sorry," she breathed, her arms lowering as if she would reach for him again as she'd done in the elevator.

Baby.

The endearment sucker-punched him. She'd called him that minutes ago, but he'd been too focused on calming down and getting his shit together to fully register it. Now, with a clear head, the word scored him from sternum to sack. Only she had ever dared to call him that; she was the only one he'd allowed. And hearing it on her lips now… No. Especially when before the incident in the elevator, the last time she'd whispered "baby" he'd been wrapped around her slender body after making love.

I love you, baby. I always will.

That had been the night before the ambush and he'd been robbed of two years of humanity.

"I was okay before I went inside." Pain, grief, and anger coalesced in his chest, the hot ball of emotion swirling, pushing against his rib cage. "But after a month in the hole, any small space feels like six feet of dirt is crushing my chest. I couldn't even stand up straight in that cell, couldn't inhale a breath that didn't taste of piss or sweat. Shut in twenty-three hours a day, I almost lost my mind as well as my voice."

Her low sigh reverberated in the room like a boom, and

the heaviness in it almost penetrated the glacial wall that encased his heart. "Killian, you have no reason to believe or trust me. But I didn't mean to harm you. I definitely didn't intend for you to be locked up for two years. Or to suffer and lose so much."

"Really?" He arched an eyebrow. "And just what did you think would happen when you called the police? That they would come out and tell us all to just mosey along?" he drawled, the familiar anger rekindling inside him.

"I wasn't thinking," she admitted in a low voice. "I was scared as hell, and I didn't think past saving you from being shot down."

Killian nodded, his gaze solemn. "But it still comes down to you not trusting me to not endanger myself or you. To you not believing I would make the correct choice for both of us. Which I did. I arrived in time to convince Jamie that it wasn't safe to go ahead with the meeting. But then the cops showed up and took us all to the station to 'straighten things out,'" he sneered, his bitterness with the police still eating away at him. "You know what happened after that." The helplessness and powerlessness that had drowned him at the time clawed up his chest. "So whatever your intentions, they were for shit." He shook his head, slicing a hand through the air. "Now unless you've changed your mind, we're through talking."

He waited a heartbeat, the silence deafening. A surge of lust, satisfaction, and that deeper emotion he refused to acknowledge roared through him when she remained quiet. He kept offering her an out, abhorring the thought that he might be forcing her. She needed to be willing, needed to want this as much as him. Because he couldn't turn back, couldn't rescind his offer. Some freak twist of fate had provided him with the perfect excuse for stroking her soft skin, sucking those pert, perfect breasts, kissing and fucking that pretty pussy without getting emotionally on the hook.

Everything he did to her tonight was about finally getting her out of his system, not love. Loving her had taught him that vulnerability and weakness weren't options. Trust in the wrong person, showing that person your soft underbelly, only meant devastation. One of his cell mates, a wannabe philosopher from Brighton, had been fond of quoting the Greek historian and general, Thucydides: The strong do what they can and the weak suffer what they must. While in prison, he'd had to suffer his two-year sentence, but when he got out, he'd been determined to never be at anyone's mercy again. Not the mob's, not the police's…not love's. As long as he kept his heart uninvolved, he could do whatever the hell he wanted. He was in control.

So after tonight, he would finally evict Gabriella from his memories, his dreams. He would be Gabriella James free.

Yet, as he stared at her loveliness, he had to thrust his fingers in his hair, loosening the bun at the back, to keep from reaching out to her…dragging her close, holding her so tight his arms grew numb. And he would still hold her.

"Lose the shirt," he ordered. Lust reignited in his gut, thickening his voice.

She stared at him, and he carefully studied her for any hint of indecision or fear. The need to strap her down and spread her wide, render her vulnerable, clawed at the underside of his skin, but if he caught even a trace of uncertainty or anxiety, he'd walk her out of The Loft and the club himself.

But she barely hesitated as she started to unbutton her shirt. Except for dropping his arms, he didn't move—couldn't move—every bit of his attention focused on the skin she exposed. He'd already had his mouth on her sweet flesh, but the need to see her lovely, full breasts with their cherry-colored tips rode him hard. Already he could feel her nipples pebbling against his tongue. Eyes fixed on her, he dragged the tails of his shirt free and undid the buttons.

"Keep going, Gabriella," he instructed when her fingers paused, her gaze centered on his chest. "Take it off. The bra, too."

As if his words galvanized her, she finished and shrugged out of the top, and the black, plain bra quickly followed. No frills. But with that body, she didn't need any. He locked down the harsh exhalation of breath that filled his lungs. Lace and silk would seem frivolous and gratuitous against the beauty of her lean, runner's body. Slender shoulders; firm breasts with large, dark red nipples; tucked in waist; flat belly; a feminine flare of hips; and long, toned legs. And then there was the neatly trimmed triangle of black hair that still glistened with her wetness.

He quickly leashed the hunger that snapped and bit at the reins restraining it. His first impulse was to leap across the space separating them, take her down to the floor, and cover her with his body before thrusting so deep inside her she would bear the imprint of him on her for weeks, months, years. But instead, he maintained his distance, desperately mending the tattered edges of his control.

Nodding toward the other side of the room, he said, "Over there."

She followed his nod, and when her eyes lit on the piece of pine and leather furniture propped next to the wall, they widened before jerking back to him. "What the hell…?"

He allowed the corner of his mouth to curl up in a mocking, half smile. "Never seen a spanking bench before? That's right. We never used one." He lost the smile, couldn't keep the facade when arousal hummed through him like a live wire. "You're about to get up close and personal with one. Unless you…"

He arched an eyebrow, offering her an out once again. Although part of him chanted, *Give me this. Please, give me this.*

She stood there, glancing between him and the bench. Finally, when he thought she would balk, she gave him one last look, then crossed the carpeted floor. The need knotting his gut went from searing to supernova. Currents raced up and down his spine, sizzling in the small of his back. His palms itched with the need to have her tender flesh under his hand. The primal urge to have her surrender all that strength and grace to his keeping, his pleasure…it tore at him.

"Wait," he rasped as she propped a knee on one of the leather pads.

He strode over to the big armoire in the corner of the room, and pulled free the bottom drawer. With care, he selected the items he would need before opening one of the armoire's doors. Seconds later, he removed a slender, small paddle and placed everything on the bed, within easy reach. Ripping the package of one item open, he gently pulled the purple butterfly vibrator free. The exact color of her eyes.

"Killian," she whispered, her wary gaze focused on the pretty sex toy.

He didn't reply, instead covered the distance between them in several short steps and knelt in front of her. Grasping her ankle, he lifted her foot and slipped it through the straps, then repeated the same motion with the other foot. Wordlessly, he slid the flexible straps up her legs and settled them around her upper thighs and hips like an erotic garter belt. This close, he could inhale her heavy, delicious scent, and he surrendered to the temptation for a weak moment, trailing his fingers through her wet slit, and eliciting a low gasp from Gabriella. She trembled above him, her slim thighs shivering, and he quickly adjusted the body of the butterfly directly over her clit.

"What's your safe word?" he asked, rising. Already, her lilac gaze darkened, and her plush lips trembled. His mind supplied the taste of that mouth—a combination of the spearmint gum she'd religiously chewed at work, the sweetness of the apple-flavored candy she had a weakness for, and her. It would be so easy for him to lean in and take her mouth, to indulge in one of those messy, wild kisses that had been a prelude to sex... But lovers kissed. And though they would definitely fuck tonight, they weren't lovers.

As if reading his thoughts, she turned her head and murmured, "Whiskey."

For the first drink she'd ever served him. And the same word and reason she'd given him when he'd asked her for a safe word years ago.

He didn't reply for several moments. Couldn't. Emotion gripped him in its fist as memories of a different time and place bombarded him. He hated the intrusion of the past on the here and now. If he was going to see this through, he needed to stay grounded in the present because the past was a trip wire that would explode in his face.

"Fine." With a grip he tried to convince himself was impersonal, he helped her climb on the bench. Positioned each knee on the slender but thick pads. Bent her over the wider plank, making sure her pelvis didn't press against the cushioned wood. Placed her hands on the second sets of pads beneath her head. After a few adjustments for height and comfort, he buckled the leather straps over her ankles and wrists, securing her to the bondage horse.

Goddamn, she was beautiful. Circling the piece of furniture, he savored the sight of her flushed face, her thick lashes fluttering over her cheekbones, soft, rapid puffs of breath breaking on her lips. Lips he would thoroughly take. Humming, he stroked a hand over her raised head, down her graceful spine, and over the curve of her gorgeous ass, coming to stand behind her. Spread for him, her plump folds glistened, and the entrance to her core fluttered as if silently pleading for his penetration. He eyed the tiny, puckered hole almost hidden between the firm flesh of her ass. It would be his tonight, too. Before she walked out of Lick's doors, he would possess every part of her.

"Anything you want to say, Gabriella?" he said, dipping a fingertip inside her, moistening the tip, and lightly pressing it to her back entrance. He didn't penetrate her, just let her feel him there. Let her know where he would be before long.

Her only response was a moan.

"Good," he praised. "I hoped that was your answer."

. . .

"Good."

The one word was rife with dark intent and rippled through Gabriella.

She closed her eyes, feeling his piercing stare on her like a physical caress. A part of her admonished that she should be ashamed, or at the very least embarrassed about being so exposed, so vulnerable and at the mercy of a man who'd made no bones about his resentment toward her. But that part had been effectively shut down by the arousal raging through her veins and lighting her up like a July 4th night sky. Had been silenced by the heart that needed to assuage some of his pain in whatever way she could. This was her penance... her pleasure. And she willingly gave it to him so that when she disappeared from his life again—probably for good this time—he might have some semblance of peace.

Not that this was all altruistic. More than her next breath, she craved his hands on her. Hungered for his cock to fill her, stretch her, brand her. Needed to experience that place where pleasure and pain mated, leaving her mindless, complete, and at peace.

Hell, she just needed.

She sensed his physical withdrawal from her. Almost as

if the hampering of her ability to touch had heightened her other senses, she caught the whisper of his steps across the carpeted floor and the tearing of plastic. Oh God, what else did he have planned for her? The slight weight of the vibrator against her sex already taunted her, and she fidgeted, trying to shift forward even the tiniest bit to place pressure on the little butterfly. If she could just ease the heavy ache…

A heavy palm landed against the underside of her ass cheek, and she gasped at the fiery sting. It radiated, pulsed, before spreading to her core, warming it. "Don't even think about it," Killian growled. "Every moan, every shudder, and orgasm belongs to me, you understand?" He rubbed her flesh, soothing it. "Understand?" he murmured.

"Yes," she breathed. "Please, Killian…"

It'd been so long. So long since someone had pushed her. Since someone had blurred the lines—since she'd wanted someone to. She wanted more, craved more.

"I know what you need, Gabriella. I always have," his rough, broken voice echoed in her ear just as a big palm swept her hair back out of her face. "And I'll give it to you."

Then the butterfly buzzed to life.

She cried out, arching her back as much as possible—which was hardly at all—as if trying to escape the whirring vibrations assaulting her clit. Electrical currents zinged up her spine, then raced back down, dancing over her asshole, and back to the pulsing bud cresting the top of her sex.

"Shh." Killian knelt in front of the bench so they were eye level, several dark strands escaping its restraint and brushing his jaw. He studied her face, as if absorbing every reaction to the butterfly's torturous and erotic ministrations. "That's the lowest setting," he said, and a glance down revealed the remote in his hand. "But we're not staying there, Gabriella." The words might have been delivered in a low, even tone, but she didn't mistake what it was: a warning.

With another stroke of her hair, he rose, and she caught a flash of golden, taut skin, a ladder of ridged muscles, and colorful ink before he disappeared out of her line of vision again. This was another form of sexual torment—not being able to see, to figure out what he intended. All she could do was submit to his care and take whatever he wanted to do to her.

And trust that he wouldn't hurt her. Physically, that is. This man alone possessed the power to wound her soul.

"You're thinking too much." A slap to her other cheek in the same spot as the previous pop. "You ready to use your safe word?" Another spank lower to the tender flesh above the bottom curve. Then another on its twin spot. "Gabriella?" he murmured, caressing the hot skin.

How could he expect her to speak when each stinging rap stole her breath? Had her sex spasming, aching? It was like each time his hand connected with her ass, the heat radiated in her core. Then add the merciless humming of the vibrator... Jesus, she could barely think, much less speak.

"Gabriella." His tone hardened, demanding an answer, and she could do nothing but obey it.

"No," she rasped. "No, I don't want to use it."

Another spank was her reward. And God, it was a reward. A biting, carnal reward. With a low groan, she lowered her head, and relaxed her entire body. Signaling her total and complete surrender.

"That's it," he praised, and firm lips caressed her ass, tracing the tingling flesh. "Good girl. I was going to use the paddle on you, but I'm enjoying having my hand on your ass way too much. I don't want to give a piece of wood that pleasure."

Two thick fingers plunged into her pussy, and she choked on a scream. Shoved so close to orgasm, she clawed at the edges of the pads her wrists were bound to. She tried to twist, to ride his hand, but she couldn't, could only receive each thrust, each curl of his fingertips against that spot high inside her that only Killian had ever located and reached. Sobs ripped from her throat as she raced toward that glittering edge…

Then his touch disappeared, leaving her gasping and panting. She locked her howl of disappointment and frustration behind her teeth, the pain of being denied again almost more than she could bear.

A cool and thick lubricant slid down the crease of her ass, and she stiffened. But not in trepidation. In excitement. In anticipation. *Oh yes. Please.* The whimper resounded in her head. Unlike some women, she'd always loved this dark, taboo possession. Because it'd been just that—a possession. A claiming. And the forbidden nature only made it hotter, made her beg him for it all those years ago. Having him slowly burying himself in the narrow tunnel, feel herself stretch to accommodate him, tremble beneath him as he rode her ass, his sweat dripping onto her back…his grunts filling her ears. Her heart thudded against her sternum, and a shiver tripped over her body.

He gripped one of her cheeks, pulled it back and worked the lubricant over her rear entrance, massaging it. More of the gel, and his finger penetrated her. She cried out, but after several seconds, the biting sensation eased into a hot glow. If she hadn't been tied down, she would've backed into that finger, but as Killian slowly fed her more of the blunt digit, she tipped her head, a soundless scream on her lips.

"Goddamn it." The snarl pierced her sensual haze. "Hot. Tight. So fucking perfect. Just like I remembered." He withdrew, then returned, this thrust smoother, easier. Still breath-stealing. "I need to open you up for me," he growled, almost, it seemed, to himself.

More lube poured down her crack, then two fingers

spread her, jacking the burn higher. And when he scissored his fingers back and forth, stretching her passage, she mewled in raw, carnal bliss. Once more, he pulled free, and she trapped a shout before it could burst from her lips. But then, the power on the vibrator jacked to a higher level, and as her scream tore through the air, he pushed one cheek back, and pushed a smooth object inside her. The flare of pain pushed back the looming orgasm, and she forced herself to breathe deep through the fiery edges of the invasion. As quick as it roared through her, the sting eased, and she moaned at the fullness of the fat butt plug.

"There you go," Killian crooned. "Beautiful. You took it so beautifully, I might let you come." Fingers brushed down her crease, tugged on the plug and sent sensations dancing over the nerve endings in her channel. Then another switch powered to life, and the same buzz that tortured her clit tormented her rear. Pulsing currents transformed her into a live wire, casting her into a realm where everything ceased to exist except the pleasure threatening to tear her apart. If only Killian would let it.

"Oh God." Shudders quaked through her, and she loosed another keening wail.

"Soon. Hold back for me, Gabriella. Don't you come until I allow it." And he rained down a series of swats, covering her ass, switching up the force, the frequency, and placement, keeping her trembling on that crumbling edge over oblivion. The stinging heat melded into one hot pulse between her legs. Thick fingers plunged inside her, twisting, withdrawing, then thrusting back inside. She skidded closer to the ledge, desperately trying to hold back, to not go over.

Pull on the plug. Press of the vibrator. Stroke of the fingers.

Pull. Press. Stroke.

Her screams poured from her on an endless stream.

Pull. Press. Stroke.

She couldn't…

"Come now, Gabriella. Now."

She exploded. Imploded. Cracked open and splintered into dozens, hundreds, thousands of pieces. Just before the darkness sucked her under, a sliver of fear pierced the shattering ecstasy.

As she'd been afraid of…she would never be the same.

Chapter Six

Vanilla and cucumbers.

Killian nuzzled the black strands, inhaling her familiar scent. Apparently Gabriella used the same shampoo as before, too. Same style of clothing. Same body products. Same safe word. Yet, she'd changed, as well. And the combination of old and new fascinated him. When it shouldn't.

He shouldn't be fascinated, curious, or even give a damn.

This was purely physical. He wanted her body, her pleasure...her shaking beneath him. That's all he needed. Not this damn stirring of memories. Not this...tenderness that wanted to take up residence like a squatter.

Yet...yet, he didn't shift her off his lap and leave the bed. Instead, he tightened his arms around her, buried his face in her hair, and breathed her in. This was okay. He could allow himself this small thing since she still slept. She'd never know, and he wouldn't have to deny.

He glanced toward the spanking bench, and immediately images of her bound to it bombarded him. Never would he be able to look at it and not see her. Not recall her, blissed out and shaking on its padded surface. Not hear her screams echoing in his head. Not feel her slick, wet heat drenching his fingers and tight flesh squeezing him like a vise grip.

No woman had ever given herself to him as freely as Gabriella. The others—they'd been erotic games, roles played. With Gabriella…it wasn't playing; it was essential.

So much had been altered, broken, between them. But this need for her surrender, her trust? It was the same. Just as vital. Just as powerful. Like then, it validated him. Made him feel worthy. If this woman—this gorgeous, independent, strong woman—could submit everything to him, then maybe, just maybe, he wasn't the petty thief with a drunk for a father. Maybe he was more than muscle for a mob boss. Maybe he was more.

How, after all that had passed between them, could she still make him feel that way? Still make him feel honored that he could care for her after she'd blacked out from the pleasure he'd given her. Make him feel important as he'd removed the sex toys from her and rubbed aloe into her reddened skin before wrapping her in a blanket. Make him feel like a protector as he held her while she slept.

Killian tipped his head back, so he could suck in air that didn't contain the scent of vanilla, cucumber, and sex. Too much shit had happened between them. Even if he could forgive and forget about her calling the police, he could never trust. He'd emerged from jail not only with a broken voice, but a broken belief in people, a mistrust that had been etched into his soul by the betrayal and abandonment of one woman.

And she rested against him, her soft breaths whispering across his skin like a gentle caress.

"Killian?" Gabriella stirred, her voice slurred with remnants of pleasure. Like a kitten, she snuggled deeper against him.

"Yeah," he rasped, dropping his arms from around her.

"I'm here."

She turned her head, her lips grazing his skin and rekindling his simmering arousal to full blast. Not that it required much. He hadn't come yet, and after having both his fingers and mouth inside and on her, his body throbbed in complaint.

Sitting up on his lap, she dragged her hair out of her face, a growing awareness quickly chasing the lethargy away. The blanket he'd wrapped around her slid from her shoulders, baring her from the waist up. Like a magnet, her full, delicate breasts drew his attention. He hadn't tasted them yet. Desire thrummed inside him, drawing every muscle tight. That would be a crime he would be rectifying soon.

With Herculean effort, he returned his gaze to her face and slumberous, lilac eyes. The humor reflected there also curled her mouth. With a small sigh, she pinched a few strands of his hair that had loosened from the band and rubbed them between her fingertips. "For the past years, I've pictured you as you were. Shorter hair. But I like this lumbersexual look you have going."

"Lumber what?" He grunted. "Is that even a real thing?"

"Oh yes." She nodded, the curl of lips wider, spreading into a smile. "There are thousands of Pinterest pages dedicated to it."

He grunted. He'd never bothered with the social media site. It seemed like nothing but a time suck and a place where people could post pictures of their cats...and apparently lumbersexual men.

"How long i—well, damn," she breathed, turning fully in his lap until she almost straddled him. Splaying her fingers wide over his pecs and shoulders, she released a sigh that sounded nearly reverent. "You're so beautiful." She traced the lines of the tattoos that stretched across his chest from shoulder to shoulder and down both arms. Ornate crosses, angels, demons, leviathans with gaping mouths...he was a walking canvas of good versus evil. A reflection of the thoughts that dominated his mind, especially after he was released from jail. Each tattoo received her attention, and just as she trailed a caress over his ink, he curled his fingers at his sides so he didn't do the same to the delicate arches of her dark eyebrows, or the elegant bridge of her nose, or the plump curves of her mouth.

"Nipple rings." She huffed out a chuckle, brushing the rings. "I thought I'd felt these under your shirt earlier. The tattoos, the piercings. They're new," she murmured. "At least to me."

Pinching one of the sterling silver hoops between her fingers, she tugged lightly. He hissed, feeling the small pull in his cock. Gritting his teeth, he rolled his hips, stroking his dick against her bare thigh. Her eyes widened slightly, a low gasp escaping her parted lips.

"What does it feel like?" she whispered, treating his nipple to another tug. "Does it hurt?"

"Yeah," he ground out, hips jerking again. "A little. A good hurt."

"Yeah," she repeated. Her hands skimmed lower, lighting up nerve endings in her wake. She trailed her fingertips over the light bruises marring his ribs. In another day or so, they would darken to the color of her eyes. Another reminder he'd carry after tonight. "Is this another kind of 'good hurt'?"

He studied her, searching her face, but she didn't meet his gaze, instead traced the mark over and over before moving to the next and repeating the caress.

What could he say that wouldn't sound just a little bit unstable? She'd already witnessed his...episode...in the elevator. The thought of appearing even weaker, crazier, in her eyes...

"Wendy mentioned you were involved in underground

fighting," she said when he didn't reply. "The fighting, the pain… They silence the demons, don't they? Give you an outlet for them." Her lashes lifted, and he stared into understanding, into compassion. The fist squeezing the hell out of his chest loosened. She nodded. "I have a lot to answer for, don't I?" she murmured.

Did she? Not with this one. Using his fists had always been his release valve. Only once he'd done it for the O'Bannons, and now he did it for himself. His sanity.

So, no, this guilt didn't belong to her. She'd been his balm, not his catalyst. But his throat closed around that admission, so he said, "Not this, no," and drop-kicked the subject for another. "Why L.A.?"

A beat of silence, followed by a nonchalant shrug. Too nonchalant. "Why not?" Her gaze dipped, and as if she couldn't keep her hands to herself, she toyed with his piercing. Grinding his teeth against the pleasure zinging to his balls, he covered her hand with his and waited until she returned her attention to him. Several more seconds passed before she sighed and shook her head. "It was the farthest place from Boston without leaving the country, and big enough to get lost in."

"Is that what you wanted? To get lost?"

Something dark ghosted through her eyes. "Once I realized God had no intention of letting me stop breathing like I asked him to after you went to jail, I figured pretty much becoming a ghost in a city where people looked through you rather than at you seemed like the next best option."

God had no intention of letting me stop breathing like I asked him to… The words rattled against his skull, and a dirty fear coated his throat, his tongue.

"What are you talking about? You didn't try to…" He trailed off, not even able to complete the thought.

"Kill myself?" she supplied. Shaking her head, she eased

off his thighs, sitting next to him, her knees pulled to her chest and held there by the band of her arms. "No. But some nights I wanted to fall asleep and not wake up. I knew you would eventually be released from jail, but for all intents and purposes, you might as well have been dead to me. After what I'd done, I'd lost you. And there were moments I didn't want to exist in a world where you didn't. Melodramatic, I know." A small, humorless smile curled the corner of her mouth. "You'd been gone about a month before I realized I couldn't remain in Boston. Not when I saw you everywhere. So L.A. it was. I packed up what I could stuff in my car, borrowed some money from Uncle Garrett, and left."

"You didn't have a place to live, a job," he said, belated worry for her settling inside him. A city the size of L.A. couldn't have been kind to a woman totally on her own.

"I managed. Found a job bartending, stayed at a motel until I could afford an apartment. I had more than you. And I've been…okay. Sometimes even happy. At the end of next month, I'm going to be the owner of my own bar. Nothing like yours," she said with a dry laugh. "But a small dive bar in Culver City. Uncle Garrett would be proud."

"That's wonderful, Gabriella," he murmured. "I'm happy for you." And he was. When they'd been wrapped around each other in bed, she would sometimes talk of taking over her uncle's bar. That she'd still managed to grab her dream… It was a testimony to her will and strength. He wasn't so much of an asshole that he couldn't be proud of her for that. Admire her for it.

"Thank you," she whispered. Closing her eyes, she loosed a shuddering breath. "Killian, I…"

"No." He jolted off the bed, stripping his opened shirt off and throwing it aside.

"Killian—"

"Lay down," he ordered, stalking across the room to the

armoire. Yanking the door open, he snatched a silk scarf off a hook. He wrapped the material around his fists, staring down at the cloth. Throwing a glance over his shoulder, he inserted a thread of steel in his voice. "Lay down, Gabriella."

After a brief hesitation, she complied and slid down on the mattress, her gaze fixed on him. Questions lurked in the purple depths, and he turned away from them. What could he say? That he'd been afraid of what she was going to say? That she was sorry again? Could he forgive her? He didn't want to hear it. Not now. Because damn if he knew what he would say in response.

He'd played himself.

From the moment he'd set eyes on her, his goal had been drowning in her once more. Taking what he'd been denied for five long years. Sex, then back to their lives. At some point—maybe the moment she slid down the wall to her knees, taunting him, or the second he'd touched her bare flesh again—the scales had started to shift. Her pleasure—their pleasure— had begun to outweigh the original goal. This night had become less about taking and more about the desire that only this woman had ever been able to elicit and stir. About feeling alive again outside of an illegal fighting ring. She'd made him come alive instead of remaining the angry shell of a man he'd been since leaving the stink of jail behind.

And he didn't want that to end. Not yet. It eventually had to; this night would inevitably lighten into day, and he would forfeit his right to touch her, bury himself inside her. An expiration date swung over their heads.

But until then, he had a legitimate reason to have her under him.

Shutting the armoire door, he returned to the bed and Gabriella. He tossed the silk scarf on the mattress, then quickly removed his pants. A soft gasp echoed in the room, and her lashes lowered, hiding her gaze from him. Just as he parted his lips to demand she open them, so he could see her thoughts, read her emotions, she opened her eyes, and Jesus. The arousal there, the heat. It seared him to the bone and twisted the dial in him from blazing to goddamn conflagration. No woman had ever looked at him with such need, hunger, or…longing.

That had to be wrong. Unlike him, she'd known where he was the entire half decade. If she'd missed him, she could've contacted him. He'd waited for her to come to him in the jail, to see him. But she'd deserted him, and that had hurt him worse than calling the cops. Even now, the knowledge throbbed like a thousand bee stings. Still, this time, he would walk away. But not until after…

"Put your wrists together and hold your arms out," he instructed, picking up the long length of dark blue material and placing a knee on the mattress next to her hip.

This time, she didn't waver but thrust her hands toward him. He quickly bound her wrists. Then, straddling her body and leaning over her, he secured the scarf around a bed railing. Once satisfied the material wouldn't loosen, he straightened and stared down at the lean, graceful, but powerful body under him. Greed and anticipation coursed through him like rushing waters finally freed from a dam.

Jesus, she was beautiful. Without warning, a fissure cracked open inside him, and a rush of loneliness poured out of him, catching him off guard. He'd missed this connection, this sense of…safety in having the freedom to be vulnerable, to be himself with a woman. Inhaling, he briefly closed his eyes. Only with her. Only with Gabriella had he been truly happy. Grief-laced anger flickered within him. Constantly being on guard, having to shield himself from possible pain was another, different prison. And experiencing that freedom right now was another, different kind of pain.

Mentally shaking his head, he refocused on the beauty

spread out before him. All that black as midnight hair spread across the pillow and tangled around her face and shoulders, spilling over her breasts. Cherry-red nipples poked through the strands, and he gently brushed them aside, baring her flesh to his hungry gaze. Her slender torso and flat belly flared into hips that fit perfectly in his hands. And then the neatly trimmed triangle of tight, raven curls. He'd had his mouth and fingers on and inside the flesh those curls hid. And he needed more. Was desperate for more of her. Needed to imprint her scent on him.

Slowly, he leaned back, cupped the back of her thighs and guided her legs up and out. With her long limbs bent at the knees, he had an unhindered view of her pink, swollen flesh. Of the puffy folds that were still damp and grew wetter under his stare. Of the small, grasping entrance that would soon stretch around him like the sweetest, tightest mouth. And... he slid his hands under her hips, lifted, and pressed his thumbs to the firm, bottom curves of her ass, spreading them. His gut clenched at the sight of the puckered and newly opened hole.

His fingers pressing into her skin, he lowered her legs and adjusted them to their original position. Once more he straddled her, and he dropped forward, his palms denting the pillow on either side of her head. For just a second, his mouth hovered above hers, and the siren's call of those lush lips tempted him. He'd told himself earlier that kissing her was too intimate, that he wouldn't cross that line. But with every breath carrying the flavor of her kiss, he couldn't deny himself this pleasure anymore. Screw the line.

In spite of the aching, desperate need insisting he take, ravage, he slowly pressed his lips to hers. Slowly parted her lips and slid his tongue deep. Slowly licked the roof of her mouth, then sucked. And tangled. The taste of her. Damn, it never got old. And he called himself about ten different kinds of fool for ever trying to convince himself he'd forgotten. That he didn't crave this. Like ripe peaches and sunshine. Like sin and every bad thing he shouldn't want. But so fucking did. That sensation of old and new ricocheted through him once more. The woman was the same, but the hungry way she nipped at his lips, danced with him—that was new. Bolder. Hotter.

Yet, it was like coming home. Like the welcome he didn't know he wanted, needed.

He feasted on her, for a moment, his control slipping as he drowned in her taste, savored each soft lick, delighted in each thrust of her tongue. Over and over, he dove between her lips, taking, giving, claiming, and surrendering.

With a growl, he wrenched away and dipped his head to her neck, delivering a hot, openmouthed kiss to the elegant column of her throat. She pressed her head into the pillow, arching her neck, and offering him more of her. Grazing his teeth over her golden skin, he sucked the taut flesh, bruising it. So when she glanced in the mirror for several days to come, she'd remember who marked her skin. Fuck, just remember him.

"Unless it's my name or your safe word," he whispered against her neck, "don't speak. Understand?" If she couldn't talk, she couldn't say anything that would derail this. He couldn't allow anything to come between them yet.

She nodded, her hips undulating between them, rubbing her pussy over the base of his cock. Electrical pulses tingled in his balls, eating at his control. Locking down a groan behind clenched teeth, he lowered his arm and tapped her thigh, stilling the restless movements.

Immediately, the shifting stopped, her puffs of breath like cannon shots in the silent room. With hunger and just a bit of wariness darkening her eyes, she watched him. That lilac gaze accomplished what her bound hands couldn't. Tested his discipline, urged him to fall on her like a starving animal and devour her. And yeah, he would—not gorging on her wasn't an option. But not yet. Not just yet...

Pushing himself off her, he balanced his weight above her. Silence permeated the room as they studied one another. With his order for her not to speak, only her harsh inhalations echoed in the air. And though with a flick of the remote in one of the bedside table drawers, he could have music pouring into the room from the state-of-the-art sound system, he didn't move.

He valued the quiet—after two years in a place where silence was a pipe dream, the void of sound was one of the sweetest melodies to his ears. And here, with Gabriella, it emphasized every gasp, every whimper, every pop of flesh, every suction of her wet sex welcoming and releasing him. And he didn't want to miss. One. Thing. He needed to etch every sound into his brain, his memory...

Splaying his fingers over her rib cage, similar to how she'd touched him earlier, he slid his hands up her torso, not stopping until he cupped her breasts in his hands. As if in benediction, he briefly closed his eyes. He hadn't forgotten, but his mind had lied to him that she hadn't felt this good. The hell she didn't. Her soft flesh filled his palms and fingers, the rock-hard nipples poking him. What had he told himself about waiting to fall on her like a ravenous beast? Screw that.

With a low growl, he dropped down and sucked her breast into his mouth. Lashed the tip with his tongue before curling around it and drawing hard. Her cry goaded him on, and he molded her other breast, flicking the peak, twisting it while worshipping its twin with his lips, tongue, and teeth. He nipped at her breast, circling the dark ring around her nipple, then raking the crest with the edge of his teeth. She twisted beneath him, and he didn't reprimand her, enjoying how she simultaneously attempted to escape his touch and crowd closer to it.

In response, he tugged, sucked, tweaked, and pinched harder. And by the time he switched breasts, she seemed firmly in the *give me more* camp. Though she didn't utter a word, her sighs, groans, and writhing told him she wanted the torment of his mouth and hands.

Use me. Dirty me. Fuck me... She'd demanded that of him, claimed she needed that from him. He intended to take her at her word. But he silently added more to that list. *Brand me. Claim me. Never forget me.*

Sitting up, he cradled both of her breasts in his hands, pushing them together. He swept his thumbs over the diamond-hard tips, and with a slow, deliberate glide, slid his cock between the mounds of flesh. A groan tore from his throat as he passed through, not stopping until his cockhead bumped her chin. Damn. This pleasure, fucking a woman's breasts, he hadn't allowed himself since Gabriella. It'd been too intimate, too personal, and he hadn't shared that connection with anyone to indulge in the act. But her...

He drew his hips back, but before his head cleared the dark tunnel her flesh created, he pushed in again. The sweat on her skin provided a lubricant, granting him a smooth ride. He grunted, repeated the slow, unhurried stroke, the tug on his apadravya sending a blast of pleasure/pain racing up his spine. *Goddamn, it was so good.* She surrounded him, and the sight of his dick riding her full breasts had lust surging through him like a hot torrent, a tenderness that he could no longer ignore riding shotgun. Several more thrusts, and his cock darkened with the blood pounding in the pronounced veins, and his balls already tingled with the need to blow. Yet, it still wasn't enough.

"Open your mouth," he half ordered, half pleaded, the rasp almost overly loud in the silence. This time when he surged forward, he bumped her bottom lip with his erection. She parted her lips, and canting his hips, he thrust between them. And groaned. Long and low.

Wet heat. The tight clasp of her mouth. The sweet glide of her tongue.

God, he'd missed this. Missed her.

Releasing her breasts, he withdrew his cock and shifted higher up her body, grabbing a pillow. He tucked it under her head, lifting her to a comfortable angle and position. She watched him, trust gleaming from her gaze, and the glimmer of it sent a fierce satisfaction barreling through him as much as desire. Curling his fingers around the headboard, he fisted his other hand around his dick and surged forward, penetrating her mouth.

"Fuck," he growled, his hand joining the first on the headboard. "I—" Quickly, he bit off the rest of his confession. But he couldn't prevent it from boomeranging against his skull. *I've dreamed about this...about you.* "Open wider for me, Gabriella. That's it," he praised.

With a slow roll of his hips, he pushed deeper inside her, and her wicked, perfect tongue curled around the tip, drew on him, flicked his piercing, then sucked on it. Pleasure streaked up his spine like lightning. He jerked in pure reflex, driving more of himself inside her on a lust-thickened groan. Automatically, she stretched for him, taking more of his cock.

"Do it again," he murmured, pulling free of the wet haven of her mouth. She released him with a soft *pop*, and the sound stroked his flesh as sweetly as her tongue. His fingers tightened around the railing as he slid back in. She sucked him deep again, tugged on his apadravya again...sent him almost shooting off down her throat.

Surrendering to the vicious need to fuck her mouth, he thrust between her lips. Over and over, filling that lush mouth full of his dick. He lowered one hand to her head, twisting his fingers in her hair. Not to hold her steady—she didn't move, just let him use her mouth. No, he just needed to touch the dark strands, enjoy the sensual caress over his skin. He'd missed it. God, he'd missed it.

"Tilt your chin up, Gabriella," he instructed. "Give me your throat. Let me in, baby." The endearment slipped from him, but the hot, wet clasp of her mouth didn't allow him the room to regret it. Not when his cockhead bumped then slipped into the narrow opening of her throat. Not when the channel reflexively tightened around him, dragging an animalistic grunt from him. Electric pulses throbbed at the base of his spine, signaling an orgasm that would no doubt render him deaf, blind, and dumb. "Again. Again."

He'd been reduced to single words. Closing his eyes, he withdrew then pressed deeper, penetrating her throat, claiming more of the passageway. But after only one more stroke, he opened them again, unable to not stare at her lips stretched wide around his cock. Other than her pussy, he couldn't imagine a more beautiful sight of him taking her. Of her wide, lilac gaze, gleaming with pleasure and trust, glistening with moisture.

"That's it," he praised, bucking into her. He groaned, his fingers flexing in her hair, over the headboard. One more entry into her throat, one more glide of her tongue, one more squeeze of her muscles on his flesh, and…

Orgasm nailed him in the back of the neck, propelling him forward. He shuddered, shook as ecstasy blasted through him with the force of a blowtorch. Cum burst out of his tip, spurting into her waiting mouth, and she swallowed every bit of him like he was the most treasured, the most delicious treat she'd ever tasted. And in that moment, he felt that way—more than wanted…cherished. Lo—

With a low growl, he shook his head, his chest heaving. *No*, he admonished himself. *Stay in the here, the now.* With trembling fingers, he hurriedly untied the silk scarf from the railings and from Gabriella's wrists. He hadn't intended to release her, but at this moment, more than being buried inside her, he longed to have her hands on him. Touching him. Caressing his skin. Stroking his hair. He didn't analyze the urge as he massaged her skin and arms, lowering them to her sides. She didn't speak, but her gaze questioned him. He glanced away from those pretty eyes as well as the swollen, damp mouth that had just pleasured him like no other had ever been able to.

With a renewed hunger twisting his gut, he moved off the bed and retrieved the butterfly vibrator, its remote, and lubricant off the bench. Setting the items on the bedside table, he climbed back on the bed and crouched between her legs. Tunneling his fingers in her hair, he lifted her head off the pillow to meet his mouth. There was no finesse in the kiss; it was wet, wild, raw, and hot as hell. Lips slid over lips, tongues dueled, teeth clacked. Her newly freed hands grabbed his shoulders, her nails digging into his skin. He growled at the bite of those nails, feeling their sting in his dick, his balls.

"Killian." She whimpered his name, the first word she'd spoken since his instructions. Would he ever get tired of hearing those three syllables in her husky, temptress voice? Ever get used to the thrill of it, the warm slide that filled him like the sweetest honey? Hell no.

He snatched the vibrator from the bedside table, and sitting back, slipped the bands and the butterfly's body in place. Ridiculous jealousy of the little toy nestled up against her clit pricked him. Shifting backward, he dipped his head and shoulders and licked a path between her soaked folds, his nose nudging the vibrator, pressing it against her. Rumbling low in his throat, he returned for another taste, loving the tangy sweetness that coated his tongue. He'd done this. He'd drawn this out of her with every touch, every stroke. Yeah, he hummed, sipping at her. This was his reward.

One last lick, and he rose over her, scattering kisses along her hips, up her belly, the center of her breasts. Unable to resist, he sucked each nipple, nipped them, before stretching over and grabbing a condom out of the drawer as well as the vibrator remote.

Quickly, he sheathed his fully erect cock. Just one lick of her addictive flesh, and he'd gone hard as a steel pipe again. A flick of his thumb, and the butterfly buzzed to life, sending Gabriella's hips dancing. He stared, mesmerized by the erotic display. With her head jammed against the pillow, her back arching, and the back of her hand pressed to her mouth, she was art. Living, breathing, carnal art. Beauty in motion.

Cupping her hips, he slid his cock through her swollen sex, moaning as her plush flesh separated for him, embraced him.

"Five years," he murmured, nudging the vibrator with his tip. Anticipation, lust, and something needier, greedier clawed at him. "Five years I've…" *Dreamed of this. Craved this.* Once more that fissure creaked open. He couldn't voice the words, but he could show her.

One more stroke that covered him in her, and he pressed against her entrance, pushing into her. He watched as he sank into her, as she swallowed him. So pretty. So goddamn pretty.

Only her beautiful face, tight with pleasure, superseded the sight.

Snug, slick heat surrounded him, squeezed his dick in a grip that damn near bruised him, but still wasn't tight enough. Small, animal-like whimpers escaped Gabriella, and each cry caressed his flesh. He thrust hard, groaning as her muscles fluttered around his length like tiny kisses. Holding still, he inhaled a harsh breath. Either that or explode, and he wasn't finished. Half of him had yet to be buried inside her. He withdrew, and the top half of his cock glistened with the evidence of her arousal.

"You with me, Gabriella?" he ground out. He waited

for her nod, and when it came, he drove forward, tunneling through her slightly resistant flesh. Gritting his teeth, he pulsed his hips, claiming more and more of her. "Open up for me, baby," he murmured. "I know that vibrator is getting you soaking wet, but press down on that little butterfly so my cock can be where it needs to be. Let me in. I need you…"

Long, elegant fingers moved to the sex toy and a long, dark groan rumbled out of her. Her other hand dipped between her legs, skated over the several inches that remained outside of her. Circling her finger and thumb around his flesh, she rolled a caress over him, sending flames licking through his veins, heating his blood.

"God*damn*," he snarled, and plunged deep until his balls pressed against her. Finally. Oh God, finally. His control broke with a snap that resounded inside his head, and he took her like a man possessed. Like a man who had everything he'd ever desired, dreamed of within his grasp and was terrified of losing it.

With a will he hadn't been aware of owning, he withdrew, and her cry of denial almost had him driving back in, finishing them both off. But he wanted more from her. He needed to claim all of her.

Turning her over on her stomach, he grabbed a pillow and slid it under her hips.

"All of you, baby," he murmured, pressing his chest to her back and nipping her shoulder. He thrust his cock between her ass cheeks and moaned, placing an openmouthed kiss on the skin he'd lightly bitten. Trailing his lips down her elegant spine, he rose, sliding his hand up the path his mouth had just travelled. He palmed the back of her head and gently pressed it. Her cheek rested on the pillow, her legs curled under her hips, ass in the air.

Snagging the lube, he uncapped it and parted her cheeks, squeezing the gel onto her puckered flesh. "Shh," he soothed when she shivered. Smearing the shiny cream on his fingers, he rimmed the entrance the butt plug had opened and prepared for him and slipped inside. The tiny ring of muscle resisted at first, and she went still. "Push back, Gabriella. Just like you did for the plug. Relax and push for me."

Leaning to the side, he picked up the remote and switched the vibrator to a higher level. A wail broke free of her, and he slid deeper inside her ass. Pulling back, he added another finger, stretching her as he worked her open.

"Press on that butterfly for me, baby," he rasped, notching his cock at her entrance. Stroking his hands up her ass, he held her apart, and slowly breached her. Gritting his teeth, he held his breath as his tip popped past the ring, and he sank inside that snug, smooth-as-glass channel.

She shouldn't be able to take him, but goddamn, she did. So sweetly. So perfectly. Growling, he rode her, watching his dick appear and disappear inside her. Over and over, he powered into her. And with each thrust, she backed into him, silently but hungrily pleading for each plunge.

Electricity sizzled up his spine, down to the soles of his feet. Her screams of pleasure peppered the air, but he couldn't come without her. Lowering his hand, he plunged three fingers into her drenched, spasming sex, hooking them and rubbing the smooth patch of flesh high in her core.

Beneath him, she stiffened. Seized. Then broke. She clamped down on his fingers, milking them. That's all it took for him. Feeling her pleasure had the orgasm he'd been holding back roaring through him with the force of a runaway train. Nailing him. Crashing into him. A seemingly endless orgasm gripped him, shook him, and he flooded the condom with his cum.

Exhaustion tugged at him, inviting him to curl up against her spine, press a kiss to her shoulder, and sleep. Sighing, he carefully eased from her body, from the tempting haven of her embrace, and made a quick trip to the bathroom to take care of the condom and clean up. Slipping back onto the bed, he pulled the blanket over her and smoothed the tangled strands back from her face.

He should've been tired, wiped out. But the more he studied the softness of her lilac eyes, the small, half smile that curved her mouth, a sense of urgency set up under his skin. He couldn't deny what had just occurred between them. A part of him longed to label it just fantastic sex. But he could no longer live in that state of denial. What they'd shared had been more. It'd been deeper. Hotter. More visceral and... profound than sex. Sex had never made him so hungry, so wild, he was desperate to mark a woman. To brand himself on her body, her memory—her heart—that she couldn't pry him loose. Sex didn't shatter him, making him feel broken but also brand new. He'd had sex with multiple women. With Gabriella, it was *more*. Just as it'd always been.

So how could she walk away from him? From them, so easily as if what they'd shared hadn't mattered. As if *he* hadn't mattered. Especially when she'd been his everything.

He lowered to the pillow, stared at the ceiling, clenching his teeth to trap the question swirling in his head like a tornado. But with his guard weakened by her, he couldn't hold it in any longer. He had to finally know.

"Why did you abandon me, Gabriella?"

Chapter Seven

"You already know about what I overheard," Gabriella started, rubbing her damp palms down her denim-covered thighs. After Killian had asked the question that had rocked through her with the power of an earthquake, she'd requested he have her clothes delivered to her. The shirt and pants were flimsy armor, but sitting there, naked on the bed, while she revisited the past with him seemed too vulnerable, too exposed in a way being strapped to the spanking bench hadn't made her feel. Especially since after she finished, she fully expected him to usher her ass right out of The Loft and Lick. She didn't need a blinking neon sign to tell her their time together was over. She'd rather not have to wait any longer than necessary before her walk of shame.

"I almost didn't call you, you know," she murmured, probably confusing him with her change of subject. She paced in front of the bed, arms wrapped around herself, although the temperature was perfect. Though she didn't glance over at Killian, who leaned against the wall, every bit of her was tuned in to him. His utter stillness telegraphed his concentrated attention, and while minutes ago, that focus had shattered her with pleasure, now it sent a wave of sadness through her. "I knew you, Killian," she whispered, all the desperation and fear for him from that night vibrating in her voice. "I knew if I told you about the double cross, nothing would have stopped you from going. And I was right. You were fiercely loyalty to Jamie Hughes and the O'Bannons, even though they didn't deserve you. Especially Jamie."

Fury burned low in her belly at just the thought of the O'Bannon family's boss. She lowered her arms, her fingers curling into fists. If the man stood in front of her right now, she'd junk punch him—with a 2 x 4.

"He used you and all the other men who were loyal to him. Saw you as his property to corrupt and send out on jobs that damaged your soul time after time," she continued, bitterness coating every word.

"I could've said no, Gabriella," Killian said, his voice quiet, solemn. "I wasn't an innocent."

"No to the man who'd been giving you money since you were a kid to take care of your father? No to the man who gave you a job, a family? You were loyal to Jamie—to a fault."

"I wasn't blind to who he was," he argued. "Not by a long shot. He wasn't some cross between a daddy and a god to me."

"Yet he had your unconditional loyalty all the same. Killian." She briefly closed her eyes. "I've said all this before, but I panicked when you rushed out of the bar. I was twenty-one, scared, and completely in love with a man who, in my mind, was running headlong to his possible death. I loved you too much. I couldn't lose you. So I called the police because it was the only thing I could think to do to save your life." She held out her hands, palms up, as if pleading with him to understand her actions and mindset five years ago. "But even now, I wish I could look you in the eyes and tell you I would do it differently. But I don't know if I would. If it would mean you standing here, alive, away from Jamie Hughes and the mob, I might make the same choice again."

Silence thundered in the room, deafening with all the unsaid regrets and accusations.

Sighing, she continued. "I found out the next day that you'd been arrested. I went to the jail to explain everything, to beg for your forgiveness if necessary—"

"What?"

She stared as Killian slowly straightened from his lean against the wall. Muscle contracted and flexed under his taut skin as he stalked toward her. Wary, she instinctively stepped back, but paused. He wouldn't hurt her—she believed that with her entire soul—and she wasn't a coward. She'd admitted her actions had led them to this point; she'd face it.

"What did you say?" he demanded in a dark, low rumble.

Frowning, she said, "I went to the jail to ex—"

"No, you didn't. You never came to visit me."

Anger flared inside her. "Of course I did," she insisted. "You should know—you turned me away. Sent the officer to tell me you didn't want to see me. I came back and tried three more times. I even mailed you a letter. But you rejected each visit and didn't write me back."

"That's. Bullshit," he ground out. "I never... *Fuck*." The curse didn't blast from him in a torrent of rage, but the soft explosion of sound. He turned away from her, thrusting both hands through his hair, fisting the dark strands. When he faced her again, stark lines bracketed his hard mouth, shadows darkened his hazel eyes. "They never told me you came. Probably intercepted my mail, too. All I can think of is either the cops wanted to keep me isolated to break me, or they just took pleasure in fucking with me. But I didn't turn you away because I didn't know you came."

She blinked. "Could they do that..."

His harsh bark of laughter interrupted her question.

"Damn right they could. Just like they sent me away on false charges."

Shaking her head, she whispered, "Would it have mattered? Would you have forgiven me?"

For a long, painful moment, he didn't reply. But when he did, his confession did nothing to ease the hurt. "I don't know. Then, maybe not. But you disappeared. You didn't give me a chance to find out. You left Boston...me. Why?"

She averted her gaze, wrapping her arms around her once more.

"Gabriella," he growled.

Worry and the need to completely unburden herself warred within her in an epic battle. Five years ago, fear had controlled her. Love had motivated her, but her fear had been instrumental in him being imprisoned for two years. She couldn't continue hiding the truth from him. This Killian wasn't the same man who'd collected debts on behalf of Jamie Hughes. This man was older, more mature, more in control. And still the man she loved. And love protected, it worried, it sacrificed, but it didn't lie. Every second she kept the truth from him was another second she lied by omission.

She couldn't do that to him...not anymore. She had to believe in the man he'd become, and also trust he would make the right decisions. That he wouldn't jeopardize everything he, Rion, and Sasha had worked so hard to build. That he wouldn't throw it all away out of a misplaced sense of justice.

"I didn't recognize two of the men from that night, but the third I did right away. You'd been in the bar with him several times. It was," she paused, mentally leaping over the cliff and depending on faith to keep her from smashing. "Michael Hughes." An O'Bannon captain and Jamie Hughes' son. "After you refused to see me—or I believed you didn't want to—I had to think about my uncle's safety. I was afraid Michael would figure out I'd been the one who'd ratted on him to you. If I left Boston, taking my secret with me, I thought Uncle Garrett would be safe, and so would I."

She braced herself for his shock, his fury, his grief. But none of those crossed his face. His hooded, hazel eyes were shuttered, the full curves of his mouth firm and flattened into a straight line. No emotion, no reaction. Just...nothing.

"Why were you afraid to tell me?" he asked. "Did you think if I knew Michael had tried to murder his father and me that I would run out of here, find him, and kill him?"

"I didn't know," she whispered. "But I couldn't risk it. I didn't have a chance to tell you then—you ran out before I could, and later... Well, later never came. And I didn't plan on revealing his involvement to you tonight. I've taken so much from you already, I didn't want to be responsible for stealing even more from you with information that would only harm you, not help. And...and," she swallowed, glancing away from him, and blinking furiously against the sting of tears. Damn. She'd managed not to cry the entire night. Just a little while longer, and she would be out of here...and free to break down. "And maybe after you issued your bargain...maybe I didn't want to go another five years without your touch. Even if it was just for a few short hours."

Heat flashed in his eyes before darkening once more.

"You didn't trust me," he said, stating a fact. She opened her mouth, but couldn't push a sound out. "No," Killian insisted, a hollow note in his voice. "You didn't trust me. Again. Back then, you didn't give me a chance to prove that dying for the mob wasn't worth living without you. And if I hadn't pushed the subject tonight, you would've walked out holding the same secret."

"Killian," she breathed. But the truth of his accusation struck her in the chest like a closed fist. He was right. Part of her hadn't trusted him. She could wrap it up in wanting to protect him, but now, with his stark observation shoved in her face, she could no longer deny the truth. She hadn't trusted him. She lifted her gaze to him. "I'm sorry," she whispered.

He didn't placate her with a false "it's okay" or a meaningless "what's done is done." Instead, he fixed his shuttered stare on her and added, "It turns out you don't have to worry, Gabriella. Michael is dead."

The words reverberated through her, gaining power and volume. Shock, relief, even anger flooded her in a crushing deluge. Stumbling, she placed a hand on one of the bed's posters, steadying herself. Dead? For how long? Had it been that night? Had she fled Boston for no reason? Had she lost years with Killian for nothing?

"How?" she croaked. "How long?"

Instead of replying, he grasped her elbow and guided her to the side of the bed. "Sit," he softly ordered, not waiting for her acquiescence and seating her on the mattress and the tangled covers their bodies had just occupied.

"Two years ago." He blew out a breath, and scrubbed a palm down his face. "We, me and Rion, decided to leave the O'Bannons. Sasha had just been shot, and he was down with starting over with us. Given how long we'd been in the gang, we thought Jamie would be okay with our decision." He barked out a cutting crack of laughter. "Apparently, we were incredibly optimistic and naive. Jamie said no. And if we tried to leave anyway, he would kill our fathers and Sasha's family since he still needed Sasha to earn money for him."

Jamie Hughes had visited her uncle's bar several times, and she could easily imagine the older man with his salt-and-pepper hair, leather skin, and booming, deep voice telling them they had no way out of the mob.

Bastard.

"We started talking about how to get out. And the only plan we could come up with was killing Jamie." A bleakness entered his eyes, and it called out to her. She twisted her fingers, clenching them on her lap so she wouldn't reach for him, offer him comfort she wasn't certain he would accept. "By taking him out, it would throw the gang in chaos. Between people trying to find the shooter and jockeying for boss, they might not care if Rion and I left, or if Sasha was no longer doing jobs for them. That would just be two less men aiming for Jamie's position or two less men to kill for it. That's what we hoped anyway."

He shoved his hands in the front pockets of his pants, his wide shoulders straightening, as if bracing himself for the rest of his story.

"We set the hit for a night when we knew Jamie would be at his office late, and he'd called in prostitutes for the boys. I volunteered to actually kill him. Rion and Sasha argued, but I'd already been to jail. Had already known that hell, and I couldn't let them suffer that. If any of us were caught, I would go back before they would. Neither of them agreed, but I was adamant. So Sasha stayed in the club for backup while Rion and I went to the office. But..." His voice trailed off, before returning harder, rougher. "But Michael had already beat us to it. When we walked in that room, Jamie was on the floor, bleeding from a chest wound, and his son stood over him, about to deliver a head shot. When he swung toward us, I didn't think. Didn't hesitate. Even though we had come there with the same goal in mind, I shot Michael." He shook his head. "So maybe what you said about my loyalty to Jamie was right. And in the end, he let us out. Either that or lose the respect of his men by not honoring the request of the men who'd saved his life."

"You wouldn't have been able to do it," she murmured. His head jerked up, that incisive hazel gaze pinning her in her place. But she met it, challenged it. "You're not an assassin, Killian. Yeah, you've done some things in your life, but it was never out of malice or just for the hell of it. You're not a monster, and only a monster would've been able to kill in cold blood."

"But I did kill. I murdered someone," he whispered. And the pain, the lingering horror in that low, hoarse voice, had her launching off the bed and crossing the short distance between them.

She wrapped her arms around him, locking her fingers behind his back, and pressing her cheek to his chest.

"You saved a man—a man you loved and resented. And from a son who was ready to murder his own father out of greed and hate." She tipped her head back, stared up at him, making sure he looked down at her. Really looked and saw the truth. "You were my everything," she breathed. "But I never looked at you through rose-colored glasses. And you never had to hide who you were from me. I saw the Killian who would leave out of the bar, ready to go on the errand his boss had sent him on. Then I saw the Killian who would later return, struggling against the darkness closing in on him. And all I wanted to do was pull you out. That was the man I fell in love with—and the one who stands in front of me now."

Her words seemed to echo between them, "love" the loudest and most jarring. Jesus. Why had she thrown *that* word in there? It mocked her, and taunted her with everything she'd had—and lost. Including Killian.

As if he would ever want her in his life again. Yes, she'd finally explained the why of her actions, but that didn't mean a what now existed for them.

Fear cascaded through her. God, she was afraid to think of a possible *what now* with Killian. At one time, he'd consumed her every waking moment—she risen in the morning, anxious to see him, ached to have him beside her when she fell asleep, was always hungry to have him deep inside her. Now, with the distance of time, she could see how her world had revolved around Killian. And that had been her fault, not his.

But the thought of losing herself in him again terrified her. The circumstances behind her move to L.A. had been tragic, but in some ways it had been the best thing for her. She'd grown. She'd claimed her own identity. She'd become her own woman. Could she sacrifice everything—her home, her bar— for him?

Yes.

The answer resounded in her, rattling her in its strength and certainty.

She wasn't the young woman anymore. And if it meant seeing the glow of love and not just lust in his eyes again? If it meant sharing her life with him? Then hell yes.

But…

Swallowing, she dropped her hands from him and shifted back. Killian watched her, tension entering his body.

"Can you…" She paused, gathered her courage and tried again. "Can you forgive me?"

"Yes."

She blinked. Rocked back on her heels. *Okay.* The man didn't mince words. Then…relief so sweet, so profound soared through her, and the weight that had sat on her chest for five long years shattered. For the first time in so long, she dragged in a deep, guilt-free breath. His hawk's gaze studied her without flinching, and she read the truth in the hazel depths.

"Thank you," she rasped. "I—thank you."

She thrust her fingers through her hair and glanced away from him. *Let it go,* a cautious voice whispered. *Be grateful, and let it go.* His forgiveness was more than she imagined she would leave here with. *Leave it…*

"Could you love me again?" *Damn. It.* The need to cringe, to yell, "never mind!" pummeled her, but she locked her teeth, trapping the words inside. She needed to know. One answer would devastate her, and the other would fill her with joy. But both would free her.

"Yes." Again that stark, blunt response, and *oh God*, her knees liquefied. Jesus. He'd said yes— "But I can't let myself love you again."

The bottom plummeted from her stomach, and with a will she didn't know she possessed, she beat back the darkness that crowded her vision. *No. Don't you faint, damn it. Stay strong.*

She locked her knees, tilted her shoulders back, and forced herself to meet his eyes—those fathomless, shuttered eyes that studied her even as he eviscerated her. She closed her own, uncaring if she took the coward's way out. Was this payback? A last infliction of punishment? Shit, the grief. The pain. It pressed down on her like tons of dirt being shoveled on top of her, burying her, stealing her air…

"I understand." Even those two words scraped her throat raw. She had to get out of here. Before she broke down and did something she could never erase. Like beg him to change his mind. Or worse. Try to change it by offering him her body… her heart. "I should go."

"Gabby."

Oh damn. Did he have to use the nickname he'd refused to call her all night *now*?

"Do you need to walk me out or can someone else take me?" She caught the trace of panic in her hoarse voice. "Please," she whispered. Screw pride.

He crossed the short space separating them and gripped her arms in his firm, but gentle hold. It was the gentle that pushed her closer to the edge. As if he had to be careful because he knew she was so fragile. And the pitiful part? She was fragile. Seconds from shattering in so many pieces, she wouldn't be able to scrape them together again before leaving this place.

Hadn't that been her fear when she'd first seen him? That he would alter her, break her? Only emotional duct tape held her together, and the ripping off of it would be hell.

"Gabby, look at me," he rasped.

She shifted her gaze to his face. Had she thought his eyes had been expressionless? No, they burned. With anger? Frustration? An emotion he'd just denied feeling for her? She shook her head as if she could dislodge the desperate, pathetic thought.

"I don't want to hurt you—" he said in that ruined voice.

"Then don't," she interrupted, jerking free of his hold. "And let me go."

For a moment, he stared at her, nostrils flaring and muscles coiled as if he were about to spring on her. She shivered, and maybe he caught the telltale reaction, because he drew back, his aloof mask falling in place.

Not bothering with a shirt or shoes, he strode to the bedroom door, opened it, and waited silently. Ducking her head, she crossed the room and exited it. Not looking back on the place where she'd found the man she'd loved…and lost him all over again.

Chapter Eight

Killian picked up the bottle of top-shelf vodka and poured another tumbler full, ignoring the questioning look of the bartender behind the glass bar. The club didn't open for another hour, and since it was a Saturday night, the place was guaranteed to be packed. But between then and now, he planned to take full advantage of the relative quiet and peace. Take advantage by getting enough of a buzz that when he went into the ring tonight, he wouldn't feel any pain. He wouldn't feel shit. Yeah, that was the plan. Feel. Nothing.

"You are being an asshole. A dumb-as-fuck asshole," Rion muttered next to him.

Killian spared Rion a quick glance before swallowing the rest of the alcohol in his glass, savoring the burn as it rolled down his throat. Only friends—the best of friends—could get away with talking to each other like that. But the knowledge didn't curb the rising irritation.

"Eloquent as always," Killian bit out.

"The truth isn't always nice or pretty," Sasha shot back, lowering to the stool on the other side of Killian. "And you're lucky. I made Rion hold off a few hours, hoping you'd come to your senses by yourself. But that was this morning, and you're still here. So fuck that patience bullshit. When we see you screwing up, it's our right to yank a rope in your ass."

"You two are really preoccupied with my ass," Killian sniped, but without much heat. Hell, how could he be mad with them? Not too long ago, he'd done the same thing with Rion. Shaking his head, he lifted his tumbler to his mouth. "Say it."

"Why haven't you gone after her yet?" Rion demanded. "Five years wasn't enough time?"

The previous night after he'd escorted Gabriella out of the club, Killian had given them the rundown of Gabriella's explanation. And though surprised, they had seemed to accept her reasons and forgiven her as Killian had.

"Go after her and say what?" Killian asked, fingers curling around the thick glass. The same powerlessness and sense of free falling that had gripped him in its vicious claws the night before tore into him again. "Lie? Tell her I trust her when I don't? Just because you two have found some goddamn happily ever afters doesn't mean everything else is going to be tied up in a neat little bow," he growled.

"I notice you didn't claim not to love her," Rion pointed out.

"Love isn't the damn problem." Clenching his jaw, he glanced away from the men who knew him better than anyone except the woman he'd rejected the night before. "That's the easy part," he murmured.

"Yeah, it's the deciding to not be a dickless wonder and letting fear rule you—that's the tough part." Sasha leaned forward, bracing his arms on the bar top. "And you, Killian, are being a dickless wonder, in case you missed my point." He loosed a hard crack of laughter. "We were there, man. We saw how she wrecked you. We witnessed it all. But we also remember how you were with her. Whole. Content. *Happy.* Between the three of us, we could count our happy moments on one hand. And you had two years of it. Yeah, she messed up. But hell, which one of us hasn't? Which one of us hasn't done shit we regret, shit we wish we could erase and start over? You and Gabriella might not be able to wipe away the past, but damn it, you have a future if you have the balls to grab it."

Killian didn't reply. Couldn't. Fear was a noose around his throat, choking him. He shut his eyes, as if he could block out Sasha's words. He'd told Gabriella he couldn't allow himself to love her again. Which was a load of shit. Because he already did...and he was afraid. The last time he'd trusted her with his heart, she'd almost destroyed him. Yes, the previous night, he'd found out the reasons she'd left Boston, left him. But the revelation hadn't alleviated the fear of the pain—the pain that had shredded him, weakened him. And the thought of enduring that bleakness again... He shook his head. No. Already the echoes of the suffering resonated within him, and they were enough to have him shying back.

"I have to go." He slammed the tumbler on the bar and practically leaped off the stool.

"What?" Rion asked, frowning at him, and Killian swore he glimpsed disappointment in his friend's gaze. "Another fight? That isn't going to solve your problems, Killian. Make the pain go away."

"Drop it," he barked. "Just..." He squeezed the bridge of his nose, swallowing the groan that rose in his chest like a ghost's wail. "Just, drop it. Please." Dropping his arms, he met his friends' concerned stares. "She's gone. And I'm fine. I'm. *Fine.*"

Pivoting on his heel, he strode across the club and out into the cold night.

A fist drilled into Killian's abdomen, driving the breath from his lungs like a pile driver. Shit, that's what the blow felt like. A steel drill to his flesh.

Ben Trainor's reputation hadn't been an exaggeration. He was a beast.

Though Killian had a couple of inches on the fighter, solid muscle bulked Trainor's big body like the fucking Incredible Hulk. He hit like the gamma-rayed green rage-a-holic, too.

Blood poured down from a cut over Killian's left eye, partially blinding him. Swiping his arm over the slice, he temporarily staunched it. Just in time to block the hand flying toward his jaw. But not well enough. Trainor's knuckles glanced his chin instead of plowing into it as the other man intended.

Damn, the pain. He stumbled back under the weight of it, knowing if he hadn't thrown up his arm, he would be flat on his ass right now. Ducking another swing, he shot his fist out, catching the fighter in the chest. He might as well have swatted a fly. Trainor didn't flinch. Instead he took advantage of the opening Killian had inadvertently left and slammed his own fist into Killian's side, damn near lifting him off the cement ground of the warehouse. Stars blinked and wavered in front of his eyes as he tried to breathe through the agony.

With a grunt, Killian shifted backward.

But not fast enough. Huge, meaty hands grabbed Killian on either side of his head, and Trainer drove his knee up. Intuition or reflex—or the damn grace of God—had Killian dropping his arms, and deflecting the blow. Deflecting but not blocking. Trainor's knee glanced off his groin.

Agony exploded low in his gut, his breath bursting from his lungs. His knees buckled, and they hit the ground. The impact reverberated in his thighs, but was swallowed up by the pain from the dirty hit. His back slammed onto the cement, and he blinked up at the dingy, gray ceiling of the warehouse, a sheet of black with swarming gold dots engulfing his vision.

God, he hurt. Every damn muscle and bone pulsed with red-hot heat. And he didn't have anything left in him. Under the roar of the crowd, Trainor's taunts and growls of "Get your ass up, bitch" reached him, as did the "Back up!" and "Calm down, asshole" of the two men Rick hired as "refs."

At this point, he didn't care if they let Trainor loose. Unlike the other nights just like this when he'd entered the makeshift ring, the fighting wasn't subduing the darkness. The violence wasn't drowning out his thoughts, his memories…his grief.

I never looked at you through rose-colored glasses.

Gabriella's voice, her words, dogged him.

You never had to hide who you were from me.

Images of Friday night filtered through his head, replacing Trainor's black, steel-toed shit-kickers and the feet of the crowd surrounding them. Of her sinking to her knees before him, a defiant smile curling her lips. Of her sleeping on his chest after so freely giving him her pleasure and trust. Of her beautiful eyes glazed with passion as he sunk deep within her, bottoming out in her tight, hot embrace.

Of her tilting her head back and telling him he wasn't a monster…that he was the man she'd loved.

Of her asking if he could love her again…

Jesus. Jesus Christ.

He wanted to close his eyes, just let everything fade away. But something smacked hard on the cement next to him, and the sound of heavy breathing jolted him from his stupor. He opened his eyes to find Ben Trainor on his hands and knees, leering down at him, breathing with the rhythm and intensity of a freight train. Obviously, he'd managed to break through the refs' hold.

"Get up and fight, or I'll end you right here, right now," the man snarled.

He pulled his arm back. Killian closed his eyes.

You were my everything.

Killian rolled. He heard Trainor howl in pain as his fist smashed down on the concrete in the spot where Killian's face had been seconds before. Inhaling, he shoved the pain radiating from his body down, locking it in a steel box deep inside him. Gathering the last of his strength, he rose to his feet. He didn't want Trainor to bring anything to an end. Not this fight, not Killian's life.

Not his chance with Gabriella.

Shaking his hand out, Trainor lumbered to an upright position and the two men circled each other.

Not like this.

"If you stop jacking off long enough, you can try." Killian grinned, which had the desired effect of enraging the other man. Trainor charged. Killian leaped forward to meet him halfway.

At the last second, Killian, grinding his teeth, dropped and, with a low, spinning side kick, swept Trainor's knee. The big man's legs buckled. His hands and knees met the cement floor. With all the remaining strength in his body, Killian jumped up and rushed him, slamming his fist into his opponent's jaw. And Trainor crumpled to the ground.

Sucking in harsh, serrated breaths, Killian waited. Praying the fighter would stay down.

Ten seconds later, Trainor remained out cold, and relief swept through Killian like a swift, frigid breeze. He stumbled once before steadying himself and stalking through the howling crowd. Pain throbbed from the cut above his eye as well as one across his cheekbone. A busted lip, swollen balls, a couple of bruised ribs, and a multitude of contusions rounded out his injury checklist.

But none of those hurts mattered as he reached the corner where he'd left his shirt and hoodie. He snatched up the clothing and hurriedly jerked them on, a sense of urgency driving him to move quickly in spite his protesting body.

He needed to see Gabriella.

To ask her forgiveness for being a coward and running when he should've been brave for her. Ask. Hell, beg.

Because it was him who wasn't. Him, who out of fear, had crushed the courage and heart it'd required to come to him. To sacrifice for him. To love him. No, he was the one who should be at her feet right now pleading with her to let him in out of the cold. To warm him.

He would be lying to himself if he claimed a small part of him wasn't terrified to love her. To take this risk. But the alternative... Returning to that desolate, lonely place, where he had to face bastards like Trainor just to feel *something*, didn't bear thinking about.

Here he stood in this dark, dingy warehouse, still fighting his way out of darkness. Still throwing futile haymakers at the demons that dogged him. He'd believed he'd gotten out, but with just her appearance shining her bright, beautiful life on his shadowed existence, he realized, no. He was still as mired in the muck of his past as he'd been five years ago. The darkness was his current prison—invisible, but as real as the steel bars he'd spent two years of his life behind.

And the person who held the key—no, who *was* the key—he'd pushed away out of fear.

He exhaled, squeezing his eyes shut before opening them to stare sightlessly at the cement wall in front of him. He had to fix this. Had to tell Gabriella not only could he love her, but he did.

And pray he wasn't already too late.

Chapter Nine

"Gabby, I didn't ask you to come thousands of miles to work," Uncle Garrett grumbled.

Grinning, Gabriella pushed down the tap, tilting an ice cold mug as beer poured out, filling the glass. Topping it off, she set it on a tray along with three other drinks. A waitress hefted it up and darted out in the crowd gathered in her uncle's bar to celebrate his birthday and retirement.

"So when your bartender called in, what was I supposed to do? Let you man the bar?" She arched an eyebrow. Not that he wouldn't have done just that. Uncle Garrett was a bona-fide workaholic and would've gladly tied on an apron and started serving beer, regardless that the building was bursting at the seams with people here to honor his eightieth birthday. Besides, he deserved to enjoy this night. Especially since it was a good one for him—he'd been able to recall everyone's names, remembered the recollections his friends brought up. Yeah, he needed this night, and her jumping in to help keep the drinks coming and the party going was just another way to show her gratitude to the man who'd been the only father figure she'd known.

And then there was the added bonus that taking drink orders and serving them up kept her mind occupied. Each hour, minute, hell, second, she didn't have to obsess over Killian and their parting of ways two days ago, meant another hour, minute, second of peace…

"Soooo, Gabby, where did you disappear to Friday night?" Wendy slid onto an empty barstool, a knowing smile curling her mouth.

Well, damn, there went that peace.

"Damn, Captain Obvious." Janelle slapped the other woman on the shoulder, elbowing into a tight space next to Wendy. She grinned at Gabriella, her eyes bright with curiosity. "I waited for you to call me with the dirty details. One minute we were waiting on you to come back from the bathroom, and then the next, Rion Ward was offering to call us a cab. Without you." She waggled her eyebrows. "So spill it, babe. Did you find Killian?"

Just the mention of his name sent a stabbing dart of fire through her chest. Inhaling a deep breath, she nodded as someone hailed her from the other end of the bar.

"Be right back," she said, escaping from her cousin and sister-in-law. Oh yeah, definitely escaping. By the time she filled the order of two pints, one Guinness, and one Jack's Abbey, she'd composed herself enough to face the avaricious curiosity of her family. "Sorry 'bout that. Did you—"

The fake, brittle smile she'd fixed on her lips disappeared into a confused frown. Neither Wendy nor Janelle listened to her, all of their attention focused on the front of the pub. As seemed to be the case with more and more people as a thick silence slowly spread over the bar until only a low hum of murmuring voices remained.

Following the direction of the others, she shifted her gaze toward the bar's entrance.

And her heart stuttered in her chest before racing like an Olympic gold medalist.

Killian.

She wanted to look away, but like a glutton for punishment, she could only stare. Take in the dark, thick hair that tumbled around the strong, sharp planes of his beautiful face and brushed his broad shoulders. A part of her resented that he could still be the image of male beauty when he'd taken a sledgehammer to her heart. But apparently, that section of her psyche bore no competition for the woman who still longed to climb him like a spider monkey in heat. Damn it.

Her uncle moved forward, greeting Killian with that pounding on the shoulder/hand clap thing men did. Only then did she tear her rapt—starving—gaze away from Killian long enough to notice the two tall men behind him—Rion Ward and Sasha Merchant—as well as the stunning brunette and redhead standing next to them.

What the hell were they doing here?

As if they all perceived her question on some weird telepathic link, all five gazes swung toward her. Aaaand so did every head in the bar.

Heat climbed up her chest and crept into her face. Picking up a cloth, she started wiping up a non-existent spill on the bar top.

"Gabby," her uncle called.

She didn't glance up from her cleaning. "Yes, Uncle Garrett?"

"Killian Vincent is here to see you," he informed her as if she couldn't see the gorgeous giant in the black, wool coat. "Claims he has something to say to you."

"Is that right?" she ground out, damn near rubbing the veneer off the bar.

"I think that top is spotless by now," her uncle drawled. "Are you going to listen to the man?"

She tossed the rag down and crossed her arms, arching an eyebrow. "It doesn't seem I have much of a choice, do I?" she shot back. Then narrowing her gaze on Killian, she snapped, "You fight dirty, don't you?"

"If I have to," came Killian's calm reply. As if he wasn't creating a spectacle that the neighborhood would be gossiping about until Jesus came back.

"I wasn't aware you wanted to fight. Dirty or otherwise." No way in hell she'd forgotten his words. They haunted her. *I can't let myself love you again.* She tightened her arms around herself, the gesture now more protective than defensive. "And you couldn't have just called like normal people?"

"I don't have your phone number. And no, a call wouldn't have worked." He stepped toward her, and the silent, enraptured partygoers parted like the Red Sea. "Because then I wouldn't be able to see your face again, even if it's just one more time."

"Oh damn," Janelle breathed.

Gabriella was struck speechless. Numb, she slowly lowered her arms, certain she hadn't heard him right. She would've sold her soul to have that said to her two nights ago. When her courage had been a healthy thing instead of a bruised one.

"I've hurt you, Gabby," Killian continued in that ruined, but lovely voice, steadily approaching her. "And it's going to take a long time before I can forgive myself for that. I know I've never been good with pretty words, but for you, I'll try."

He neared the bar, and Wendy and Janelle scrambled out of the way, making room for him. If her heart wasn't cracking down the middle, she might've found it comical.

"You were always the best part of me. If you didn't know that, then it was my fault because I should've told you every day. Making sure you knew how important you were to me should've been my first priority, my job. You told me I wasn't a monster. That's because of you—you were my conscience, my humanity, my heart. If it weren't for you, I might've become something unrecognizable, but you reminded me every day who I was... Loved."

This isn't fair. For someone who believed he didn't have lovely words, he was apparently a fast learner and doing a bang-up job. *You were always the best part of me.* She blinked against the sting of tears, ordering herself not to let one drop spill over. If he believed that, then why had he pushed her away? Why hadn't he wanted to love her again? Her heart refused to stop adoring him—it would sooner cease beating. But her mind... What if they were just pretty words, and one day he decided forgiveness was beyond him? That loving her was a mistake?

I don't know if I'm that brave.

Silence filled the room, and she could feel the eyes on them. Hear the soft sighs of the women, and the rumbled approval from her uncle. But only Killian filled her vision.

Killian's bright hazel eyes, hot and focused on her.

Killian's firm, unsmiling mouth and the small cut on the corner of his bottom lip.

Killian's big body, tight with tension.

Braced for rejection.

"Uncle Garret," she whispered.

But in the utter stillness of the bar, he must've clearly heard her, because he yelled out, "Yeah, Gabby."

"Can we borrow your office for a minute?" she asked.

He snorted. "It better be only for a minute. Don't make me have to come knocking. And Killian Vincent?"

Killian turned and faced her uncle. "Yes, sir?"

"You hurt my girl again, and old and feeble-minded or not, I'll whip your ass before God gets the news, you understand me?"

"Uncle Garret," Gabriella hissed, mortified. *Jesus Christ.*

"I understand," Killian replied, and though his shoulders didn't shake, she caught the vein of humor in his voice.

"Killian." She reached across the bar and touched his arm. "Could we take this to a more private place?"

He nodded, and moments later they headed toward her uncle's office, the weight of the partygoers' speculation and greedy curiosity on their backs. As she twisted the knob on the door, Rion Ward called out, "A round of drinks for everyone. On me." She closed the door on the cheers.

"What are you doing?" she blurted out, leaning against the wall. Hell, she needed the support because her legs were doing a piss-poor job of holding her up.

Killian slid his hands in the front pockets of his black pants, and studied her. The dark waves of his hair emphasized the beauty of his golden eyes, and yeah, she sounded like one of those flowery romance novels, but she just wanted to fall into them.

She pressed her spine against the wall. There would be no falling into eyes, arms...or anything else until she had answers.

"This," she waved a hand toward the door, "public declaration thing isn't exactly you."

"No, it isn't," he agreed. "But I was desperate." He glanced to the side, and she caught the tic of a muscle along his jaw before he turned to her again. "You make me desperate," he rasped. When she dipped her head, he shifted forward, lifting an arm toward her, then after a brief hesitation, dropping it. "Gabby, please look at me."

With obvious pain abrading his already rough voice, she couldn't *not* comply.

"You've been fighting again," she whispered, her fingers itching to brush the fresh-looking cuts on his cheekbone and above his left eyebrow. "Demons?"

"Yes. But of my own making this time," he murmured. "What I said out in the bar was true. Rion and Sasha... They were my brothers, but until you, I didn't know tenderness. I didn't know what it was to have someone smile like the sun had risen just because I walked through the door. My father didn't care if I came home, much less if I'd eaten, or if I didn't feel well, or if I was hurt. But you did. For the first time in my life, I was someone's world, and you were mine. So I held on tight…too tight. I lived in fear that you would be ripped away from me. Or that one day you would realize I wasn't worthy of your adoration and heart. I was terrified that one day I would walk into the bar, and you wouldn't smile." He chuckled, the sound serrated, dry. "And what I feared, I created."

He shook his head. "After I went to jail, I was wild with pain and anger. But I was also relieved." Gabriella frowned, and a corner of his mouth curled into a humorless half smile. "I know, it sounds crazy, right? But underneath everything else? Yeah, relief. Because the shoe had dropped. I could stop wondering when the end would happen. And I would also never feel love and the agony of having it ripped away again. In a life that had become chaotic, that I could control. But the moment I saw you again, I realized I'd been bullshitting myself. In that instant, I knew I couldn't let you in again because you had the power to take me back to that dark place that I'd promised myself I wouldn't return to. I convinced myself having your body again was enough, that I could be satisfied with just sex, but as soon as you walked out of Lick— no, *before* you walked out—I knew I'd fucked up."

He moved forward, eliminating the distance between them. No hesitation. No permission. This was the man who had taught her body to sing to the special, erotic tune he set. The man who made her body implode with pleasure. The man who owned her heart.

Pinching her chin, he stroked the pad of his thumb over her bottom lip. "You asked me if I could forgive you. Yes. You asked me if I could love you again. The truth is, I never stopped. Not loving you would mean not breathing."

Those tears, those damn tears she'd promised she wouldn't shed... Well, that ship sailed as one, and then another, rolled down her cheek. With a low murmur, he wiped them away.

"You have a life in Los Angeles, and I don't want you to give it up for me. Just..." He pressed his forehead to hers. "Let me be a part of it. We can make Boston and L.A. our homes, or you can stay in L.A., and I'll live bi-coastal. Or I'll give Rion and Sasha my part of Lick and help you build your dream." He brushed his lips over her brow. "Please," he murmured. "Let me share your life."

"Only if you let me share yours," she whispered. The last barrier she'd erected around her heart cracked, the many fissures giving way under the pressure of the love and hope that filled her chest. Her soul. For the first time in five years, she felt...whole. Complete. Shivering, she leaned into his mouth, his kiss, his big, sheltering body. "We'll figure out the details. As long as we're together, we can make anything work."

A shudder worked through him and vibrated against her. "Tell me, Gabby," he demanded.

"Do you know how much I love hearing you call me that?" She cupped his face between her palms and tilted his head down so she could graze his mouth with hers. Scatter kisses over his chin. "Don't ever call me anything but Gabby, okay?"

"Whatever you want, Gabby. Now, tell me," he murmured, his tone urgent.

He didn't have to clarify; he needed from her what she craved from him... "I love you, Killian Vincent. From the age of nineteen, you've been my everything, and you always will be."

With a low groan, he crushed his mouth to hers. She eagerly parted her lips, curling her tongue around his and cherishing his moan, and the press of his erection against her stomach. He was hers, and she let him claim her, brand her as his.

Forever.

"I think we've been longer than a minute." She smiled into the kiss. "Unless you want to face my uncle's wrath, I think we should get back out there."

Killian laughed, and for the first time since reuniting with him, the sound contained humor…joy. Brushing another caress over her mouth, he clasped her hand in his. "As long as we do it together," he said, giving her back her words, her vow.

She squeezed his fingers. "Together."

Epilogue

Killian rose from the dark blue leather couch, a glass of champagne in his hand. Music from the club reflected off the glass of the VIP room, white privacy curtains helping to mute the noise. Glancing around, he couldn't help but smile at the warm glow of satisfaction that settled in his chest. The people he cared about most surrounded him. Rion and his wife, Harper. Sasha and his fiancée, Corrine. And of course, Killian's reason for breathing, existing...

He extended his hand toward Gabriella, and returning his smile, she wrapped her fingers around his and stood beside him.

"All right," he announced. "I know you're all wondering what the secrecy is about."

"It had crossed our minds," Rion drawled.

"I was being patient," Harper said, throwing a chiding glance at her husband of nine months. "Unlike some people."

Rion leaned forward and whispered something in her

ear that had the lovely brunette blushing and clutching his friend's thigh.

Gabriella snorted. "I think we better get • this announcement going before we lose those two."

Laughing, Killian held his glass of champagne higher. "Everybody grab a glass of champagne. We're celebrating."

"Is this about Gabby's restaurant being named one of L.A.'s top ten dive bars?" Sasha asked, rising with his glass in hand. "Congratulations, sweetheart." His friend leaned over and placed a smacking kiss on Gabriella's cheek. "We saw the article online and couldn't be more proud."

After only a year, Gabriella's place—simply called The Dive Bar—had become one of the more popular establishments in the Culver City, CA, area. She and Killian traveled back and forth between the east and west coasts, so she could remain hands-on with her restaurant. And yeah, they were racking up the frequent flyer miles, but the jet lag and constant—sometimes relentless—pace was worth it to see her make her dream come true. As long as he could share in it, like he'd asked in her uncle's bar a year ago, he was happy.

"Hear, hear," Corrine cheered, clinking her glass with Gabriella's. "You know, Gabby, if you decide to open a Dive Bar here in Boston, I would recommend it to all my readers. Girl, you'd clean up." Corrine, a sports columnist for *The Beantown Globe*, a popular, local online magazine, had a huge following, and Killian didn't doubt one recommendation from her would have people packing into the bar.

"I love your belief in me and my entrepreneurial skills, but let me get past the first couple of years first before I think about opening a chain." Gabriella grinned at Corrine, hugging the redhead. The three women had become fast friends, and while he, Rion, and Sasha were thankful the women they loved got along, the trio could be downright scary when they conspired against the men in their lives. Which was often.

"I almost shit a brick when that article came out, but nope, that's not why we asked you guys here." Sliding an arm around Gabriella's shoulder, Killian pressed his lips to her hair, savoring her sweet, familiar scent. Thanking God he could inhale it every day. "Gabby and I made a pit stop on the way home from L.A. yesterday." Pausing, he reached in his pants pocket and removed a diamond ring. He slid it on her left ring finger and kissed the jewelry that symbolized his love and commitment to this woman. "We stopped in Vegas and got married."

Stunned silence permeated the glass-enclosed room for several long moments. Then shrieks of joy—from Harper and Corrine—and lower, but no less enthusiastic, murmurs of congratulations momentarily eclipsed the muted music.

Joy that he could share this moment—his happiness, his bright future—with not just his woman, but the men and women he considered family, filled him to the point of bursting. This—his brothers, the women who adored them, completed them, this business they'd built together, the life they shared—this was peace. Hope. What they'd fought to free themselves from the mob for.

It was perfection.

"See?" Sasha nodded his head toward Killian and Gabriella. "See how simple eloping is? How happy they look? How...unstressed?"

"Can it, Merchant." Corrine narrowed her eyes on him, jabbing her champagne in his direction. "You want to explain to my mother why she can't plan our wedding or see her daughter walk down the aisle?"

Sasha gave an exaggerated shudder. "Fuck no. Never mind."

"Pussy." Rion snickered.

"Hey, have you seen her mother with her Irish up?" Sasha demanded. "Screw you. She's scary."

"Hey." Corrine slapped his arm, grinning. "That's my mother you're talking about."

Chuckling, Sasha lifted his glass high. "To Mr. and Mrs. Vincent. Wishing you many years together. No one deserves it more than you two. Love you."

A chorus of well wishes followed the toast, but as Killian sipped the sparkling wine, he noticed Harper didn't have a drink.

"Harper?" He arched a glass, glancing from her to Rion, and then returning his attention to the slim brunette. "Everything okay? You don't like the champagne?"

She smiled, tipping her head back to meet her husband's gaze as he wrapped his arm around her shoulders and pulled her close. "No, it's not that. I just have to forego alcohol for a little while."

He frowned as Gabriella said, "Why would you... *Holy shit.*"

"You're pregnant," Corrine shouted, shoving her glass into Sasha's hand before launching herself at Harper. The redhead embraced Harper, and seconds later, Gabriella joined in.

Thrilled for his friend, Killian crossed the floor and drew Rion into a tight hug. As soon as he stepped back, Sasha dragged him into one.

So much joy. So much promise and hope.

A year ago, they'd been fighting to find their feet in the new world they'd created. But it'd been one devoid of love, of family other than their brotherhood. But now their future stood in this room with them.

Love had changed them.

Had saved each of them.

And every day was a gift.

Acknowledgments

To my heavenly Father. Without You, none of this would be possible. You're my strength, my hope, my perseverance, and my faith whenever mine takes a bit of a beating. Thank You, and I look forward to partnering up with You on the next one. I love being the backseat driver.

To Gary. You're my concrete evidence that God loves me. Thank you for your unceasing support, love, and kid-wrangling. It was your faith in me that set me on this path, and I love you for it.

To Tricia. You left this world for the next while I was writing this book. I was derailed a little, but then remembering who you were — are — gave me the strength to keep on. I know you're up there directing the angelic choir right now. And giving them their note, because no one *ever* has the right note. :)

To Tracy, aka Super Editor aka boss of the Montoya Mob. :) Thank you for your unending patience and humor. At the sake of getting sappy, you've been a blessing to my career, and I just SO appreciate you for your knowledge and experience, your willingness to share both your enthusiasm and your advocacy, and for being you. You are like The Beatles of editing. Montoya Mania. Haah! I'm having T-shirts made up...

About the Author

Naima Simone's love of romance was first stirred by Johanna Lindsey, Sandra Brown, and Linda Howard many years ago. Well, not that many. She is only eighteen…ish. Though her first attempt at a romance novel starring Ralph Tresvant from New Edition never saw the light of day, her love of romance, reading, and writing has endured. Published since 2009, she spends her days—and nights—creating stories of unique men and women who experience the first bites of desire, the dizzying heights of passion, and the tender, healing heat of love.

She is wife to Superman, or his non-Kryptonian, less bulletproof equivalent, and mother to the most awesome kids ever. They all live in perfect, sometimes domestically challenged bliss in the southern United States.

Come visit Naima at www.naimasimone.com.

DESIRING RED
a *Dark and Dirty* tale by Kristin Miller

Choosing a werewolf mate who'll be with me until I croak? Pardon me while I take some time to think on it. But a steamy encounter before the final ceremony changes everything. Reaper, the Omega's eldest grandson, is fiercely loyal, scorching hot, and built for pleasure. I've only just met him, but I *need* him like no other. By pack law, Reaper can't have me until the Alpha makes his choice…but Reaper's never been one to follow the rules.

SHAMELESS
a *Playboys in Love* novel by Gina L. Maxwell

People say I'm shameless. They're right. I like my sex dirty. It takes a hell of a lot to tilt my moral compass, and I always follow when it's pointing at something I want. Especially when it points straight at the one girl in all of Chicago who's not dying for a piece of me. She's all I can think about, and that's a problem, because she wants nothing to do with me. But I've seen her deepest secrets, her darkest fantasies. Now I just need to show her how good it can feel…to be shameless.